DAWSON, FIELDING, 1930-200
THE TRICK : NEW STORIES /

1991.
37565009117069   CENT

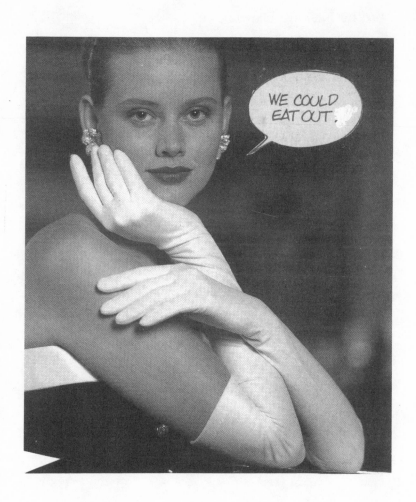

Also by Fielding Dawson

Stories & Dreams:

Krazy Kat/The Unveiling (1969)
The Dream/Thunder Road (1972)
The Sun Rises Into the Sky (1974)
The Man Who Changed Overnight (1976)
Krazy Kat & 76 More, Collected Stories 1950–1976 (1982)
Tiger Lilies: an American childhood (1984)
Virginia Dare, Stories 1976–1981 (1985)
Will She Understand? New Short Stories (1988)

Novels:

Open Road (1970)
The Mandalay Dream (1971)
A *Great* Day for a Ballgame (1973)
Penny Lane (1977)
Two Penny Lane (1977)
Three Penny Lane (1981)

Memoirs:

An Emotional Memoir of Franz Kline (1967)
The Black Mountain Book (1970)
The Black Mountain Book, *A New Edition* (1991)

Poetry:

Delayed, Not Postponed (1978)

FIELDING DAWSON

THE TRICK
NEW STORIES

PHOTOS & COLLAGES BY THE AUTHOR

BLACK SPARROW PRESS ■ SANTA ROSA 1991

THE TRICK: NEW STORIES. Copyright © 1991 by Fielding Dawson.

All rights reserved. Printed in the United States of America. No part of this book may be used or reproduced in any manner whatsoever without written permission from the publisher except in the case of brief quotations embodied in critical articles and reviews. For information address Black Sparrow Press, 24 Tenth Street, Santa Rosa, CA 95401.

ACKNOWLEDGMENTS

The author is grateful to the editors of the following magazines, wherein many of these stories first appeared: *Blind Date, Bombay Gin, Brief, Carbuncle, Conjunctions, Heaven Bone, In This Corner, The New Censorship, River Styx, Shiny, 3 X 3, Taos Review, Transfer, Just Buffalo,* and *Witness.*

Thanks also and beyond measure to Walter Washington, for permission to use his three poems, and to James Welsher, for permission to use "The Rose."

"Celery Stalks at Midnight" written by Carl Sigman, copyright © 1941 by Robbins Musical Corp. Copyright renewed by George Harris and Will Bradley 1968.

Black Sparrow Press books are printed on acid-free paper.

LIBRARY OF CONGRESS CATALOGING -IN -PUBLICATION DATA

Dawson, Fielding, 1930-
    The trick: new stories / Fielding Dawson; photos and collages by the author.
    p.   cm.
    ISBN 0-87685-819-1 (cloth): — ISBN 0-87685-818-3 (paper): —
ISBN 0-87685-820-5 (signed cloth):
    I. Title.
PS3554.A948T75   1991
813'.54—dc20   90-23890
                                                                   CIP

In Memory of Seymour Krim

"You must know by now that we are exciting but unreal animals in the world's disbelieving eyes. And even though we have electrified millions and millions of individuals across the waters because of our unique playground of blood and technology, and the music and film that sock it globeward, we are at the point of being a luxury they can no longer afford. Don't doubt it. Some of their best minds hope away the night praying that we could by some new post-Jesus miracle be penned into our own silver stadium of dope and bourbon and fun orgies on top of the biggest atomic generator in the world, with small bombs going off as each of us comes, plus all the other groovy Texan things we enjoy. As long as we were prevented from ever again mingling with paler, saner peoples."

I'm the American Murder-Man
1973

Life will not be the same.

Contents

The Trick

THE TRICK TO BEING intuitive is to catch the hunch, grab onto that little feeling, bring it up into consciousness and do what it says. For example.

You're at the track. In the 6th race it's Hoodwink at 40 to 1. You get a prod, an inner nudge, a hunch, that little feeling saying *Do it! That's the horse!*

Speak it. Yes! Say it out loud!

"I'm gonna put one hundred bucks on my horse *Hoodwink*!"

"Your horse?" the lady with you will ask.

"The winner," you'll brag. Certain.

"Yeah," she'll sigh. "Well, go do it, we need that money!"

"You bet! Stay here, I'll be *right back*!"

But if you *don't* follow that little feeling, and do what it says, you're gonna stand there, maddern a hungover hornet, down $4,000 as Hoodwink walks into the winner's circle. How often have you heard it?

"Goddammit, I had a hunch! Why didn't I *bet* it?"

"Because you're a dummy," she'll say.

Pissed *off*! Um *um*!

*   *   *

A man had an appointment with his dentist to have a temporary front bridge removed, and a new, permanent bridge put in. The temporary had been installed some years back, by his former dentist. The new dentist, while at work, had often poked around that temporary, murmuring, with frowns, it looked *okay, but it's got to be taken care of*. So the day

9

came and it was. Temporary removed, the dentist discovered a tooth — a tooth, like a fence post in a clearing — where they expected to find barren gums! But the tooth was abscessed, the gums were rotten. Tooth had to come out. He x-rayed. See? Right there on the negative. The patient looked. That dark area.

Ah yes, the patient sighed, and began to perspire. With chrome-plated pliers in his hand, the dentist clamped the lone tooth, wiggled it from side to side which at first caused an ache but as dentist got serious, began twisting the tooth, pain intensified moans and groans ow into *aw* into OOOHHH OOOOOWWWWW. Dentist injected a novocain hit which didn't take, gums too rotten, pliers wrenched, *unhn, aw,* but didn't kill him and the tooth was out. A clink as it struck the worktray, where dentist tossed it saying,

"The gums around the remaining left and right front teeth need to be trimmed. I didn't expect this." Pause. "I'll give you some more novocain, and do that next."

Waiting for the drug to take effect, the patient and dentist had a dialogue, in which the patient, note — *twice* — got a nudge, a certain feeling telling him *not* to talk so. *Be still!* Which he ignored. Hm.

The dentist liked his patients, saying he had a good practice and enjoyed seeing them, present company included.

"If you didn't like your patients," his patient said, looking up from the chair, felt a sudden inner twitch, don't *say* what you're about to! *Don't!* Felt an odd gap, as the words came out: "That wouldn't be good."

"That's right," the dentist replied.

"So it's good that you like what you do."

"If I didn't I'd, well, I—"

"You'd—"

SHUT UP!

"—make mistakes."

WRONG! *ALL WRONG!!*

"Even people in the dental lab," the patient added,

10

perhaps in haste? As if to cover up, hm? "If in the dental lab, the guy there didn't like *his* job, think of *those* results!"

"That's right."

"In any branch of medicine."

"Yes. True. Any branch."

"It involves all concerned."

"It's a group effort," the dentist said. "Feel a little tickle in your lip?"

"Um hum."

"Tongue?"

Nodded.

"I'll begin."

So the patient, in some anxiety, asked,

"You're going to do some periodontal work?"

"Just around these two teeth. It won't hurt." Pause. "It'll mean just a couple of stitches." But he was already at work, and it was going fast.

"Rinse. Be careful. There's a lot of blood."

The patient followed the chair going forward, turned and unloaded a whole mouthful of blood into the swirling water in the round sink. Blood soon gone, but its deep redness, and quantity! Jesus Christ! With all these black chunks and globs of decay, long streams of red and pink spit, well he used his paper bib and got cleaned up and followed the chair back. Dentist continued until he said rinse again, patient did, but on the next,

"Rinse," patient forward, something that was trying to get through to him did not. What was it? He spit out a lot of blood again, reached for the paper cup of water to rinse, and did rinse but the rim of the cup was not just imprinted with red, but dripping blood! He turned the cup—his head down, face above the sink, mouth drooling fresh blood into the water, turned the paper cup and sipped from a clean edge, rinsed, sipped more water to rinse more but the rim was wet with blood, so too the water. Soon the entire rim, and the

11

sides of the cup, as well as his fingers, and his bib, bloody!

He muttered, numb, blubbering lips hanging, "I need another cup of water." Silence. Bloody hands began to tremble. Where was the dentist?

Where had he gone?

Was he there?

The patient dared not move from the sink, even though something was wrong. Peering to his right, trying to look over his shoulder saw nothing. Empty doorway. Out of the corner of his eye to his right, in a desperate sidelong look, in the very corner of his vision saw the dentist, standing, facing the rear wall.

"I cut your lip."

Talking to the wall.

Something banged in the patient's brain: booming, *boom boom boom* until a blaze of light made it clear: *You shouldn't have said "mistake": it gave him the idea! He isn't one of us! He doesn't know!*

But the dentist was so angry at himself he couldn't speak, until he returned to the scene, gave the patient a new bib and more water but not a new cup. Called in his assistant, together they cleaned the man up, daubing hard the patient's numb, bleeding lip, to halt it. Did. And prepared to put stitches in both the lip, and gums, while finding his voice, dentist explained the difference in threads, as well as the nature of the cut, very sensitive area, the lip, profuse bleeding on the slightest cut. Would use a special, very slender thread, while the thread for the gums would be heavier — somewhat — and in a zip zip zip style, like a spider, he had the cut sewn up — a two-stitcher — soon ditto gums. Gave patient an extra packet of square 2″ cotton pads, in case he bled anew.

*   *   *

It just had to be. As the days went by, until he would see the dentist again, that is, until he did he became convinced the dentist had by mistake cut his lip because he predicted it, so the dentist had to do it.

The dentist wasn't so . . . sophisticated. He did not hear voices. Also, the dentist was there and not there, *See? One of those!* So, the dentist had not yet realized his own voices, nor the intuitive little hunches, so he was in a mystic way deaf, and numb to his predictive powers, which was why he did as his patient bid, he cut his lip, by mistake, as he had.

Had he known, in an inner mystic way *do not cut him . . .* but he was deaf, and his patient had to tell him, for he as yet didn't know the trick of listening to himself and perhaps others, in the silent ways.

*　　*　　*

Walking over for the second visit, anticipated the drilling and preparation of teeth for an impression and a new temporary bridge, but knowing as sure as horse races that that experience — the mistake — last week, had taught him that it was up to him to take care of the dentist, to be good to the dentist, and perhaps all involved in the medical profession, surgeons in particular, to defer to them, be nice, be just a little of the masochist to please The Other in them, who was ever alert, and knew *lots* of tricks, innocent though they might be, the one who was there, the one who never went away, *wanted* to cut, and his trick was to get the patient to want it too, and to like it. That was why there was something peculiar about this patient. This man who wore the Jesse Jackson button. Who had a way of knowing things before they happened, and reacting so fast he put words in the dentist's mouth before the dentist knew what to say: he made the dentist feel fey, as if something had been taken, but what? What was it? What could his patient take from him?

The patient was doing in his mystic way what mystics do in these things, the patient took himself with him as he departed, and he left nothing but a bloody mess for the dentist to throw away, preparing for another patient. He cleaned up. But the man with the black man on the button had gone. Of him there was nothing left, because he did not want to leave anything for the dentist because the dentist had gotten enough, until next week, and until the week after that until the whole job was over, he would let him have no more. Yet the dentist felt as if something had been taken from him, which he had had for a while, he had had that man in the chair and he had cut him, and as the man walked out afterward, the dentist was in his way lost, and confused in a childish feeling, as to weep, and scowl up into the eye of God, at the nature of things, in primitive language, in this unexpected way, he felt betrayed, nay! *Hoodwinked.*

In Red

THE DOC HAD SAID the finger—the little finger on the
patient's right hand—would, following surgery, be smaller,
but straighter. He held the finger, stroking it while looking
across the examination table, at the patient.

"Okay." Patient angry.

In revulsion at finger, telling doctor cut the blasted thing
off.

Oh no, no no, Doc said, there was too much feeling in
it. Yes, knuckle locked. True. But he could cut or arrange
a mystery to leave the finger a little shorter, but straight. Er.
Straight*er. Straighter.*

Doc said. Him. The real doc, the surgeon, not some
flunkie.

The operation an interesting story, and afterwards,
the next day, for patient stayed overnight, the next morning
doc came in with a few other docs, all bright-eyed as doc
pulled up a chair and sat down, saying finger had not come
out as straight as he had hoped, nor was it any shorter,
but it was *better,* murmuring, as he removed bloody understand bloody, soaked and soggy bandages it was *much* better.
Dabbed around, cleaning around the stitches and wrapping
hand anew in clean gauze, adding a splint, which held his
forearm in a sling from his shoulder, to the tips of fingers
peeking out, small, pink survivors, wiggling at command—
doc said,

"Good."

Rose to his feet with a smile. Had thin lips, thin, sharp
smile as he explained fusion, middle knuckle to the other docs
who beamed and nodded, walking toward the door. Window

15

to their left: a building across the street reflected in doc's glasses as he spoke:

"It looks good. Get dressed and go home. Call my office tomorrow, set up an appointment for next week." Poignant look followed by a smile, sweeping exit all docs, white cotton belts, buckles dangling, billowing coattails, very serious. Finger better than before, it was, and doc was right, although it was just a bit straighter, same length well doc had done what doc thought best, and he understood doc saying it hadn't come out like he'd said, meaning patient had a gimpy finger for the rest of his life. Doc knew. A top pro. Doc. A *good* person, *a fine doctor* patients came from around the world, remember the prize fighter from Philly, with his trainer? Shades of Damon Runyon, hey the doc was tops, no kidding. The *best.* Which patient understood, in the game patient forced to, if patient didn't, how could what doc did have the meaning it did to doc? Why not say it? Doc was a wiseguy! Patient had a wide range, seeing this wiseguy in action like off camera dialogue with younger, student docs, or associates *in the hand trade,* lent but one more detail to the whole picture — the patient would understand, as part of the process, the drama of medicine.

After a follow up checkup one afternoon, doc slapped the manila folder, with all patient charts and information inside — whap! — over the patient's head.

"Take care!" as he rose to his feet, so too the patient, amused yet astonished: in one look, above the thin smile, doc's eyes real bright behind their glasses, in a wink, a little glitter of was it *warning?* Am I mad? thought the patient, in understanding, but right before his eyes seeing an expression: *You are not! It is me! All* me! Of course this was doc's way, at work and at play, all doc's doing, patient relevant? Subject: matter. Dialogue impossible, none. Hi. Hi. Patient forced to be choosy, very very the few words permitted, awed, defensive, to speak, ah, words that the doc *might* hear, and which ones, and how many, *would* doc hear? Based on how

16

doc had responded in the past, who wanted to speak to him at all? It was so simple, cold, and simple: doc had cut him off from the doctor.

Nurses, other docs, staff even former patients fond of saying he's a *good* doctor meaning person, skilled, just in that way it could be said doc is skilled, *not* a good doctor or person, basic, understood that doc had to hurt people to make them better which for any reason—personal or professional—doc had his life too, dig, but he knew which patients understood, he was going to hurt, so good doc went into illusionary reversal, skilled, good, nice guy, white, cold, razor twinkle smile, why he even *dressed* in white mmm in—invisible, in the beginning, telling patient he'd insert steel pins into finger, to keep knuckle secure during the healing process, patient wouldn't even know they were there. Okay. Patient heard him, heard those words, and understood. Looked at little finger. Wiggled it.

"Okay."

So. After the operation there they were, in follow-up, post op visits, doc clapped the x-ray onto the lighted viewing screen. Both men saw mechanical flotsam, silver steel bars, adrift in photo-negative galactic space.

"Space ships," patient said.

"Huh." Doc.

Towards the end of the patient's visits, one of the pins shifted, began on an angle to stick through skin on the outer side of finger, just above first knuckle. Slightest touch painful, getting worse. Pressure made the whole area pink, with a small white dot in the skin, raised, a white dot of braille.

Made an appointment, scheduled late in the day, so the sun was floating down behind tall trees, on the avenue, early twilight waiting in the waiting room, longhair f.m. music, wooden, upholstered chairs lined the wall, grease spots on tan wallpaper above each chair, in a row, under framed museum reproductions of modern French masters so with screams of pain from doc's *inner sanctum,* art may serve a purpose. A door opened, receptionist's head peeped out: patient's name called. In he went. Saw the doc who looked at the finger, saw the swelling, pushed on it, and as the patient cried out, made a serious smile, with that glow in his eyes. Laid out a broad white towel, gauze pads. Scalpel appeared in one hand, a can of ice-spray in the other which he pointed, pressed *zzzzzzzzzzzzz* back and forth on the side of the finger, an ugly, tummy growling feeling for the patient, driven by curiosity watched doc make an incision as chrome pliers appeared, with shiny porpoise snout, mouth opened, entered bloody incision, gripped tip of steel pin. Patient groaned. Gripped his right wrist with left. Doctor murmured warm, tough doc sympathy *he knew* oh *God* patient moaned, tips of pliers inside finger clicked, skidded off silver pin's tip, doc pushed the pliers in, tried once again, missed. Wiped finger off, wiped instrument clean, went in again, patient closed his eyes as snout nosed in, gripped the pin, missed, but got it. Grip held. Patient lowered head. Pliers slipped off into blood, finger meat, patient helpless: bowels began to move as pliers gripped, patient ground his teeth, moaned, and clenched as the pin slipped out from bloody finger into air. Twinkled silver. Out!

"There," with a smile. Dabbed, and bandaged finger. Patient sat jaws set, near choking, muscles tense, doc—

"It'll be fine. You won't know it had been there." *Hm!*

Both men stood. Doc smiled, they shook hands, waved farewell, and the man in white strode in utter confidence to another patient in the next cubicle, leaving his other one alone, one more, as in a play, or a dream as the fella with the bandaged finger fought his bowels, staring at a white wall, as that lucky old sun made his way down the sky, without a care in a twilit world.

Patient took a step, took one more, right hand shaking so held it with his left: as animals, comforting each other. Bit his lip. Fought tears. Walked across a carpeted floor. Out into and along a quiet corridor, stained wood walls lined with

18

framed honors, step step toward the inner, and outer street doors. In red. Up three steps. Pushed open first door. Stepped toward the second, turned knob, shoved it open, step step, out on the sidewalk. Free. Turned east, bandaged right finger held by left hand, up across the front of his blue Navy jacket. Collar up. Eyes in slits. Glare of sudden streetlights, step step step. Toward the river.

Any Questions from the Balcony?

for Charles Dart Jr. M.D.

1.

IN THE SMALL, white-walled cubicle, seated and facing each other across a small desk with a soft white cloth on top: a middle-aged male doctor, and his middle-aged male patient — post-op visit — to have stitches removed from the palm and the little finger of his left hand. The thought of feeling them being removed, just the thought, made the patient nauseous. There were a lot of stitches.

The doctor, a hand specialist who had performed the operation, wore a smile, and gazed down upon the patient's hand, fingers curled, palm up, as though it were a separate organism. Doctor had an expresson of accomplishment, and, having stripped away bloodsoaked and crusted, pus-gummy dressing, and laid bare the naked, ravaged torn-up battlefield-hand crisscrossed with stitches like barbed wire — doc picked up hand, held it in his own hands, looking down at it.

"Let's see," he smiled, as the patient cringed as the doc lowered hand onto cloth (his touch felt good), "good," doc murmured. "Open as far as you can."

Patient did: mottled red skin bleached white, causing the red trenches, in taut spidery stitches, appeared more from a frontline MASH unit — or from a butcher's locker — than a civilized medical cubicle ah hm, haa, hmmm.

"What a mess." Patient.

Doctor smiled (rimless) glasses twinkling (that kind of face) as he opened a small, stainless steel tray, and removed

21

chrome snippers from boiling water. Front of snippers blunt, like a cardinal's beak. Patient, with sinking heart, pleaded:

"You're not gonna take 'em *all* out—?"

"We'll see."

Hm hm hm.

In doc's steady hand the sharp snout of the steel beak dug into a red-edge-crusted gutter of pus and blood to the first stitch: snip, tossed, like a dead mosquito, onto the white cloth, beside a pile of a halfdozen small, cotton squares, on standby. JIC (Just In Case).

The pain had been instant, sickening. Hand had retreated but, held firm by doc's free hand, helpless. Hand trembling, like a lamb, as with learned skill, just as pain began to ease doc dug in again and removed the second stitch, tossed it onto the cloth and as the pain eased, steel beak dug into blood for the third one. Patient closed his eyes.

"Aw Jesus."

"I don't mean to hurt you," doc offered, snip toss, snip toss, poised above where he had in surgery cut deepest, a gory rip with two stitches, and the words ringing in patient's ear, redbird's beak tunneled down under, snip toss snip toss, patient's eyes misted.

"Goddamnit, that *hurts*!" Ground his teeth. "That thing's *sharp*!"

Snip.

Snip.

So *that* was it! The doc didn't mean to hurt him, he just hurt him! Yeah! Right, plain old you *bet* unh-huh, understanding based on years etc. of experience. This was the beginning of a vital stage in the healing process, everybody knew aw man *everybody* knew that, but that was not *it*. *It* was patient being there to accept pain, the inevitable hurt for the inevitable reward: a healthy hand! Ha ha, ha ha hahaha HA HA HA! The teaser! Happy to take it for what it is for the end result, come on out and enjoy it! So does the doc! It doesn't hurt him! He knows what he's doing! He doesn't mean to hurt you, he just does!

22

What could patient's hand — poor lamb — do? Trapped, held by doc's own!

Snip.

Snip.

First fact: doc was *king* in his world and doc said he didn't mean to because he was above it, away from it, although of course *aware,* he didn't, didn't feel it didn't feel the *pain* . . . the many hands he'd worked on, and watched get better and better until all healed, *he* knew. And maybe at first he felt the pain, but hand after hand, passing through his hands, under his knife, he got used to it. Maybe he didn't feel much of anything, except for personal stuff, gratification, with his skill in his fingertips and a sense of completion, the touch to patient's hand, not like the great docs: feeling the flow of connection with another hand.

Meaning the patient had no chance for an intuitive, alert relationship, and any dialogue would be categorical, efficient, from doc, but desperate, even fugitive, from the patient: ever unsure, suspicious, cringing and frightened, eyes on the doctor's hands . . . but wasn't this normal? Understood? In clinics, hospitals — doc the romantic hero, the king, the saint, *never* wrong *always* right?

Snip.

Snip.

The patient's stomach worked its way up his throat, and his forehead beaded with sweat, teeth clenched . . . doc snipped zig-zag across patient's palm, snip snip snip along around hand's edge snip up along outer edge of little finger snip, up along the edge snip to the second joint, tossing the pieces of black thread, growing pile of dead skeeters on white cloth. Doc placed snippers on the towel, and lowered or guided patient's hand, down onto the towel, palm still up, and pressed the finger down, until it was flattened, and pale as the patient's face, and eyes, wide, watching the skin stretching, gaping, raw cuts split, as they widened in ugly gut-turning, sickening pain, the

23

surgical cuts held firm: no blood, just a little pus, no mess, or muss.

"All the way down," doc said, with a note of menace. "*All* the way down. And out." Talking to the finger. "Stretch. Strrretch," pushing down hard, "that's good, good—" and taking hold of finger, pulled it, but patient's arm jerked, hand twitched, leaped free! Cupped snuggled held safe in patient's other hand as patient said, to the astonished doc:

"No. No more. It hurts too much. Later I will, but not yet."

"That will delay therapy."

"Not much, and if so, so what?"

Doc smiled, eyes veiled, and nodded. "Begin using lotion, get that brand, Intensive Care. You'll see pieces of skin flake off, so keep the skin soft, and flexible, with the lotion. Use it often."

"Okay."

And, bandaged up—much lighter, happier, patient walked along the sidewalk toward and at length down into the underground where he stepped on board the next ear-splitting mechanical dragon that would take him home. Depressed. Doc had patted the back of his hand, said see you next week. With that complicated doc-look that made his eyes twinkle and hard to define, above a small smile, otherwise expressionless. The boss. Who never did anything that let you forget it. And it went altogether without saying that the patient had to keep doc happy, set himself to be malleable in doc's hands 'cause that's the way the medical game went: anyone in the doc's hands related to anything doc did or would do, as sure as doc's knife and patient's flesh. So in tune with doc's will and ego, patient's humility became the fulcrum: this was doc's show, guaranteed to hurt, before doc's exit toward another patient while the previous one got well. Doc hadn't learned the humility the great docs feel, to share with the patient, and heal within it, feeling as a distinct part of his commitment. No. Thus pain and patient were liberated, to be

24

taken as they pleased, as a masochistic honor, in the accepted, professional doctor/patient relationship.

2.

Right hand. Not left.

Slight infection at the cuticle. Little finger. A few weeks after surgery on that hand, and that finger. Stitches removed . . . same stage, actors, and fool: Depuitren's Contracture. Doc had put in some pins, to fuse the knuckle, informing the patient he "wouldn't even know they're there."

So, in that little, white-walled cubicle, same table, doc took the finger. Felt around.

"I think it's one of the pins." Patient.

"I think so too." Doc. "It's on top. I can feel it."

"It drifted."

Doc felt it, nodding, ignoring patient's accurate comment, as the patient looked at him.

"Don't press too hard, it hurts."

Doc nodded.

"What'll we do?" Patient. "It might get infected." Sudden flash of doc, cutting finger open again, going in with those pliers . . . felt sick. "Shall we wait and see?"

Did doc feel patient's hand tremble?

"Yes," doc said. "Soak in warm water. Let's wait and see."

3.

Infection did set in. Patient phoned doc, but spoke as always with the receptionist who spoke with doc, who told her to set up an appointment, tell the patient to have x-rays made and bring them along. Information relayed to patient.

Patient did as instructed.

So.

In that cubicle again, same table. Doc stroked the little finger, right hand. Nodded. Placed the x-ray on the viewing screen, switched on the light, and there they were: tiny steel pins, silver on black, floating inside the finger, a couple, three? in an x-formation through the knuckle. Doc patted finger, made a dimpled smile, said,

"Good. They can all come out."

"All? But I thought—"

"Set up a date with the hospital, ambulatory, same day surgery. Receptionist up front will help you."

"The hospital!" Patient. "Surgery!"

"Yes. The knuckle is fused."

"B-but I thought y-y-you'd do it *here*!"

"Oh no," doc laughed. "I don't want to kill you." Hmm um. Hm.

Patient in shock *did not speak*: get me in the hospital not to kill me, just a little hurting fun, like you did with the stitches, eh?

Doc's eyes raised. Fixed on patient's.

"You don't remember, do you?" patient asked. "After you put the pins in, saying that I 'won't even know they're there'?"

Doc angry. Smile a grimace.

"Until they tell you," he joked. Eyes flashed.

Patient unnerved. "Don't you remember cutting my finger, and taking the older pins out?"

"Yes. It wasn't easy working with that knuckle." Doc looked through his own face, from a new distance, as he rose to his feet. "Set up a date for surgery."

Patient's lips parted, hearing a voice—

Say it!

Doc and patient looked at each other.

Patient rose.

Tell him!

Patient snarled, "*Thanks,*" eyes blazed: "*buddy.*"

Doc's head lowered, gazed at and picked up patient's

26

manila folder—his chart. Wanted out of that room, you could *see* it, so out he went. Smile fixed on his face looking not very funny, under what was in his eyes.

But patient did as ordered. Set up the surgery date with doc's secretary, patient furious doc was so cold, offhand, cursory. The woman saw it as she filled out forms, and phoned the hospital.

4.

Back in the O.R. Again

In and out same day meant *nothing but surgery.*
A no-frills job.
Face up, on his back on that table in white in the white smell under that large cupped blue-white dream, hearing voices around him. The doc-voices. Doc-people, in a slow, slow pale green cotton motion, as he recalled. While saliva filled the back of his mouth, a taste of vomit rose in his throat.

Outside in sunshine, he swallowed both, and fury waned. There were, after all, a few weeks before he went in, and as he'd learned, he would live his life until that day. With that thought, paused, and looked around.

Across the street a historical museum, large, ornate, looming, with a vast green lawn. Benches, children with their mothers . . . A gas station on the opposite corner, next to a small bank. A telephone booth. Hot dog vendor. Bright yellow cabs lined up under trees. Cabbies taking a break, sat around on benches, in shade enjoyed a bite with a cuppa coffee. Birds chirped.

Warm. Blue.

5.

In pajamas and robe, in a wheelchair, was pushed into the waiting room where he was transferred on to a mobile stretcher, and after a long wait, wheeled into the Operating Room. Passing the doc on the way, sitting on another stretcher, exchanged glances. Hi. Hi. Smiles. Inside, the patient transferred on to the operating table, stretcher parked nearby. He laid back, face up, staring at the fascinating glowing moon-lamp above as bodies in pale green gowns and white masks chatted among themselves, hovering around, and near him. Hooked up the IV. Right hand stretched out perpendicular *all* the way out, resting on a hard surface much like the shape of an ironing board with padding and sheets. Lots of talking.

This was it.

Having been there twice before in less than a year, the patient had no illusions. Difference being the finger would be given a local anesthetic, and he would be awake, alert for the action, and after a recovery period would be wheeled upstairs, get dressed, phone his sweetheart and be waiting in the lobby as she came through the door.

The floor of the hospital where his clothes were (in a locker in a very pleasant room), was for the ambulatory patients: walls with posters, vases of flowers on tables, children's drawings and paintings, nurses helpful, cheerful, all bright, and colorful to slip and hide you away from what was going on down below, in the meat lockers: 1C, 2C, 3C — numbers for the operating rooms: C for Cellar. The men in white, with their knives. And sleeping meat.

6.

On his right little finger, right behind the cuticle, a large blister, swollen, infected, leaking pus and lymph. A dull, splotchy bagging thing, halfway to the second joint where,

28

under the skin, in front of the pins that had aided the fusion of the knuckle, two other pins pointed straight ahead, like tiny arrows, pushing through the skin at the base of the blister.

Doc had talked with satisfaction of the job, in his small white room, in his nice little not so little office on the plush side of town. But the patient, together with doc, looking at the x-ray mounted on the viewscreen . . . his heart sank into his guts giving him heartburn, looking at what doc wasn't seeing: the pins had, from the area of the knuckle, entered the rear of the blister, in the pale ghost of its x-ray outline were right there — just *about to puncture it.* He felt a sharp pain in the finger, glanced, or tried to, and saw or thought he saw glint of needle, injection, *hurting him,* perspiration on his forehead, startled. Helpless. Grunted. *Unh.*

"Local anesthetic." Doc.

Patient closed his eyes. Doc could have said, *This is going to hurt.*

Another injection! Hard, slow steel needle pushing in underneath deep, deep needle in. In. *Unnnh.*

"There." Pause. "Doctor Kooter?"

Patient strained to see, saw a young doc tilt a bottle of mercurochrome on latex gloved hands, this was Kooter, young doctor K, raise the patient's right hand and with a pair of hands as heavy as iron, drenched and scrubbed the ugly acrid rustyred stuff on patient's fingers, hand and forearm, and with both hands rub hard, up and down, scrubbing the member clean until he got to the little finger, and thinking as he scrubbed not about what he was doing ran his hands over the tips of steel pins, the patient yelled

"OWW!"

and sat up.

The docs swung round.

Glanced at each other.

Looked at the patient.

Who said: "That HURT!"

"Okay," doc said, with a nod to Kooter, who handed

the patient's hand to doc, who gave it another injection that hurt, not quite like before, and patient resumed position, face up. Eyes wide. Doc:

"That'll do it."

As the anesthetic put finger to sleep, young doc Kooter began putting a tourniquet around patient's upper right arm, just down from the shoulder, without speaking so patient wasn't sure what to do, like in rehearsal. Kooter holding the length of narrow rubber tube in one hand and patient's arm like it was a dead fish, with his other trying to kinda lasso it. Fish didn't know what to do. Fish wanted to help, so did the patient, as Kooter thrashed around, and at last got it done. *Whew!*

"Good," doc said.

A green sheet rose like a wave over the patient's upper body, and onto a frame fixed on the table, by the right side of his face, where it stayed, like a tent, so he couldn't see, which disappointed him . . . but they explained about germs, patient understood, and unable to see the action, or even feel it, he recalled the face of the young med student Kooter, at work with Fish, and, in part captivated by what he saw, he took a brief hiatus from surgery.

For Kooter was spoiled. His lower lip protruded Meese, Edwin Meese-like, as he had wrestled with Arm (Fish). Never dare (why?) to ask his patient for help. They don't teach that in med school, unh *unh*. Didn't Kooter — anyway — didn't he know how? Even after the embarrassment, causing patient such pain — who could have guessed the anesthetic hadn't taken? A freak! Never happened before! Ah, hm hmm *but it may again!* Unheard, unheeded. If it matttered, Doctor K would know the answers or, so it seemed.

Blue-black moviestar curls, dark, dewy lashes around almond-shaped eyes, soft cheeks, dimpled chin, face and body dusky, baby smooth, and rosebud lips a pale, shadowed pink: snow-white teeth. But as he had tangled with Fish and the rubber tube, his face had darkened: he was not getting his way

30

and doc was watching. Didn't like that. Didn't get his way how he wanted it he might get angry, ask mother what *that* was like. Pretty nostrils flared, handsome features creased, silky eyebrows knit.

In truth doc, *the* doc, paid no attention, not that he hadn't seen, for Kooter was this week's newest student, and Kooter wanted to do what doc did without you could see he didn't want to learn, day by day in life's schoolroom, toward mature discipline and skilled control no. Kooter wanted the meat on the table before him, all fixed up and ready to cut.

In this rumination the patient missed what the docs, nurses, roving interns and suchlike were saying among themselves, and felt a jolt, like the sudden tug of a stem from an apple —

"What — !" (patient)

"The last pin's OUT!" (a nurse)

Presto! Done! Cleaning up and clearing away began . . . patient on the one hand happy it was over, happy he had memorized young Kooter's face, yet chided himself for missing what they all had said, what a chance he had had! How rare! Thus paid attention, looking this way and that, at each and all as he waited to be wheeled out, watching the others in green as they stood, speaking or moved with deliberation or just sat on other tables or stretchers in the operating room, the patient understood: *it had been boring to them,* the young ones for sure, and — there! Kooter and doc together, talking. Doc had *that smile.* Watch out Kooter! But know-it-all-K MISSED it, and in regards to a point of reference, a particular concerning hand surgery, Kooter quoted a passage from a text, praising the text, his eyes bright, showing the older, top professional how smart the kid was: Kooter's eyes shone.

"I'm not keen on that book," doc said, deadpan THERE IN THE O.R.! Kooter so certain he'd be praised, so convinced that his face fell, he *fought* for control. Doc walked away.

31

So sure of instant approval, and praise — gratification, Kooter so destroyed he couldn't ask the doc *why,* and doc didn't care. Which meant, to the patient, who was being wheeled out into the corridor, Kooter might well be a patient hm hm like a lotta docs, and looking at his hand saw a Band-aid, a Band-aid? Shocked. Only a *Band-aid?* And asked doc, hey —

"How long should it stay?"

right by the doorway.

"Ask Dr. Kooter," doc said, with a vicious little gleam in his eye, above a cool, sardonic smile, hm? Any questions from the balcony?

Patient turned and looked back across at Kooter who, his head down, as angry and glum as a boy can be, answered with full authority:

"A day or two."

"Of course," patient agreed. "It'll come off of its own. I see . . ."

Kooter raised his head, eyes stricken: looked long across the O.R. at doc, who had turned away, to talk with a nurse about the next patient.

7.

Before he took the elevator down to the lobby, a nurse handed him a prescription for a painkiller, just in case (JIC). He paid no attention, and without looking, slipped it in the inner pocket of his sportscoat. If the doc had put nothing more than a Band-aid on the finger, there wouldn't be any pain. He was right. Few days later threw it away, but just before he did, he looked at it again. The handwriting seemed odd, wondered if they taught docs in medical school to write so that nobody but a pharmacist could read it, which meant maybe in pharmaceutical school they were taught how to read docs handwriting. Maybe there was a code. Anyway, it was

32

Kooter who had written the prescription, so the doc was teaching the kid the works, from bottom up, eye tripped over the signature, having assumed spelling would be K-o-o-t-e-r, it was Cutter, C-u-t-t-e-r, as in cut it out.

Had Kooter/Cutter's dad or granddad, or both, been docs — surgeons, and changed the pronunciation?

Well well, thought the patient. What a funny, unfunny world. *Who Framed Roger Rabbit?* A Toon judge. See?

8.

The finger healed so fast it was a wonder. Ten days after surgery was scheduled for a post-op visit, cocky as could be made his way crosstown and took a bus up, along tree-lined streets passing a bookstore, art galleries, fancy boutiques, restaurants, an art museum and city park.

He had made up his mind to tell doc, or ask him, what *he* thought about Kooter/Cutter. So taken — seized by the mystery, eager to talk with the doc.

Inside with other patients he waited, and waited. And waited, almost rehearsing his lines: *Why didn't Kooter ask me to help him? Why was he so heavy-handed in scrubbing my finger — having assumed the anesthetic had taken, without testing it. Why hadn't anyone told me the injections were to be given and that they would hurt? Didn't doc think Kooter/Cutter was compulsive, competitive, arrogant, insecure, spoiled and childish? And what about the pronunciation of that name? Cut is cut, not koot!*

Patient's name called.

Into the *inner sanctum* he went. To wait until doc finished with two other patients, in other, side by side cubicles. He went over his lines with such conviction and faith that he overlooked doc's standard aloofness, professional cool and lack of response to *anything any patient thought about saying.*

Doc came in with an Oriental woman — a future lady doc. Doc held the patient's chart in his hand, which he opened, and briefed her on this patient. Doc sat down. She remained standing, gaze intent. Patient already seated put his hand on top of the table, palm up, opening and closing all fingers. Doc real pleased.

"Terrific," he said. Big smile.

"There's a slight tenderness," patient began, showing the side just down from the cuticle.

Doc nodded.

"Who was the younger doctor?" patient asked.

Doc looked at him. Blinked.

"During the operation. Cutter? He assisted you."

"Kooter. Yes."

"It's spelled Cutter."

"Kooter," doc said. "He's right here," as young doc Kooter entered the room, patient's eyes going wide, pupils popped, lips parting, jaw hung. Kooter smiled down on the patient.

"Hi."

Soft, beautiful voice. Youthful. Shy. Demure, his body soft, with a feminine glow. Dark blueblack curls tumbled . . . each eyelash sparkled with dew, casting a shadow over his eyes: his gaze, tender, seductive: soft round dusky cheeks as his slight smile held, as rosebud lips parted, glimpse of pearly teeth. Tip of red tongue.

"Any questions?" doc asked.

"Well, I—unh, are you sure, this is—him?"

Knowing it was, but amazed *Kooter was here!* Doc laughed. The woman smiled.

"Maybe you don't recognize him out of surgery," doc joked, and rising, stuck his hand out.

Patient stood up. The two men shook hands.

"Goodbye," doc smiled.

"Goodbye?" patient, in disbelief.

"Stay away from doctors," doc smirked, rather beside himself in amusement, an expensive ball point pen circling a word on a small, printed diagnostic report (Patient Dismissed). Handed it over.

34

"Give this to the receptionist before you leave."

And the three left him behind as they walked out, and around into the next cubicle. The patient, not knowing what to say, did what doc told him to do, so before he left, handed the paper to the receptionist, and walked out one door, up steps to another door, which opened onto the sidewalk. Stepped outside.

Stood, looking around.

Watched the sun send shadows of trees across the rich black asphalt avenue, where yellow cabs parked, and their drivers sat on benches eating hot dogs, and talking, out in the world, the big outside world of other people, where life went on, as the former patient leaned against a plain brick wall making every attempt to laugh, as tears ran down his cheeks. Yet he wiped his eyes, and glancing at the back of his hand saw a streak of mascara, smudge of dusky tan makeup. Baffled, and perplexed, he put on sunglasses and made his way through underground tunnels home, where he looked in the mirror and saw Kooter.

*   *   *

Why? Why *Why?* he asked himself, next day and next, and the day after that until ssssssssss BANG!
Bam!
Recalling his reaction to Kooter. All those questions he wanted to ask doc *about* Kooter, fat chance he'd have. Asking doc. Doc wouldn't answer his telephone unless his receptionist took the message. Doc? Who couldn't *talk* without announcement. Doc who was cool, remote, aloof, meaning that the patient, in going up to see doc to ask him those questions was as dumb as Kooter quoting a text doc frowned on, and like dummy Kooter, dummy patient was stunned, because both had set it up for doc to knock 'em down, a favorite sport of doc's, because doc was *boss* and he would let you know it —

35

wasn't it doc who said, 'Stay away from doctors'? Ha ha ha
. . . Didn't *doc* know? Ha ha ha, ha ha HA HAHA HA
HAHA HAHA HA HA . . .

Edge of the City

SCENT OF BRINE. Garbage. Gas.

Deep, hooting growl of tugboat.

Dark, deserted street. Midnight.

Footsteps.

Man. Head high. Hands in jacket pockets. Jacket buttoned. Collar up. Walking. Step. Step. Step.

Eyes narrowed. Lips set.

Footsteps. Turns, sees another. Young. Black guy. Leather jacket. Silver studs. Jeans. Walking faster. Catches up.

"Hey! You afraid of me?"

"No."

Black man slides a finger across his upper lip, asks:

"Your name Don?"

"No. I walked out on my girlfriend."

"Oh. Yeah. Sorry."

Black man stops. Watches him: head held high. Hands in jacket pockets. Collar up. Walking toward a distant streetlight. Walking. Step. Step. Step. Scent of brine. Garbage. Sudden silence.

Edge of the city.

Noon of the City

AT NOON, in the center of the city near the train station, a man stood on a corner in a crowd in a *lot* of traffic, waiting for the light to change. Honk honk trucks, beep beep cars, saw out of the corner of his eye, it was *her*! Turned! Looked! Yes! Running, full figure rushing toward him wow wow ambulance she'd covered every front page in the world for a generation beep honk legs pumping loomed long, *honnnnk,* fast! Step step before his very eyes! Wow wow honk beep flying down the sidewalk in black! Beep. High heels, silk stockings, skirt not so short as the ones she'd made fashion in the 60s beeeep honk but still short! Shirt and pleated black silk jacket, hood tight round her windblown black hair, head high honk, hands fists toward the next corner beep, huge dark glasses glossy shine covered half her face step step beep honk step *wow wow* beep watching her run on her strong slender legs, oh boy *still* classy beep, red-rimmed mouth open, laughing as she ran on by beep beep, step step wow wow honk step beep through a crowd near the train station honk, in the noon of the city.

Why Not?

OUT OF COLLEGE long enough to find a job. Had that young, informal look: waiter, bartender. Stage hand. About six feet. Clear brown eyes. High forehead. Soft, light brown hair combed forward into a point. Broad shoulders. Flat, hard tummy. Blue t-shirt. Jeans. Sneaks.

Standing in the subway car speeding down the tracks. A small lady asked a question. Grand Central? He explained her transfer, with directions. His voice nice. Light. Firm.

She smiled. "Thank you."

As the train took its long turn, and pulled into Grand Central, a man seated near the opposite door noticed two clasped safety pins, attached to one of the front belt loops of the young man's jeans — wondering:

Why two?

Until it dawned.

Telephone Telephone: Freelancers

For Frank

YOU LOST IT!" she cried. "Why?"

"The afternoon job," he said. "I still have the other one
. . . it was my fault."

"What did you do?"

"They hired me to proofread, but wanted someone who
could write."

"Copywriter."

"Yes. They asked could I? Stupid me said no."

"You should have lied."

"I know. After all these years with these people, I tell
the truth. Can you believe it? But it's not all bad." He paused.
"They asked if I had lost a lot of work by taking the job and
I said yes, so they gave me four hundred." Pause. "A week's
pay."

"Not bad."

"How are you doing?" He'd gotten her an opening for
a new job.

"They're just beginning, have one client. One dictionary.
They're ordering pencils."

"It's *that* bad?"

"I had to bring my *Manual of Style*."

Sharing amusement. Freelancer jargon for a new ad firm.

"No. They're nice. It's okay. I mentioned the three-hour
minimum."

"Good. What did they say?"

"They're too new for that commitment, but agreed to
twenty dollars an hour."

"Ter-RIF-ic!"

"Yeahh," she sighed. "I think I'll stay with it. I can walk to work, too, which is a break."

"I'll say. Who are *they*?"

"Partners. With one secretary. And one layout person, a woman in her thirties." She described the partners.

"Bill Chang's over six feet, and—

"CHANG! Is he cute?"

"Well . . . in a way."

"Does he know Dorothy?"

They laughed.

"I don't know," she answered. "His partner is married."

Sounds of big city traffic.
Fading.

"Hello?"

Talks All Day

SHE TALKS ALL DAY about you-know-who, with those false eyelashes, my goodness, no wonder he's miserable."

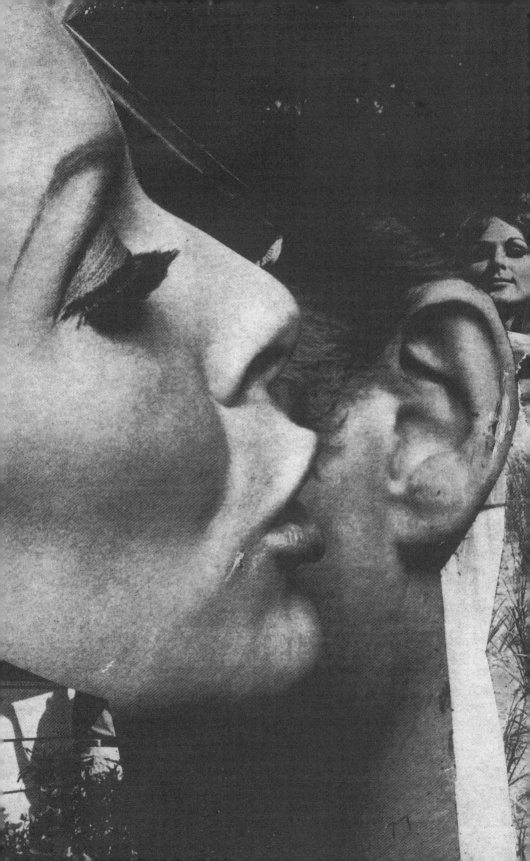

The singer finished the set to the enthusiastic applase óf an audience with an untrained ear as Michael Dunne dashed across the set of *Star Trek,* a dra dwarf a hip a hippie dra dwarf in beard, beads, bangles and lanky hair round a gaunt and haggard face dashed across the barroom floor to the bar and and stood up on the rail, and held his hands high but the bartender knew what the hip hippie dradwarf dwarf wanted, his big hands, he had big hands, the dwarf had big hands, and the bartender placed a drink in each. Michael Dunne raced back across the set. The singer sipped Scotch on the rocks at the far end of the bar, gazing down into her drrrrink: she couldn't sing, but the illusion was bew, was bew bew gorgeous and she was, too . . . low cut black dress, pale oval face, the nightclub pallor, eyes dark and lips bright red parting, white teeth touched ice, amber fluid went down her throat. Glanced at a man standing beside her, whom she didn't know nor did he know her, but having heard her sing. The hippie dwarf joined friends who were not dwarves at a table, cut to Kirk, and Spock, as the man at the bar fell into conversation with the pale beauty of limited song.

47

In Room 119

for Richard and Mei-Mei

ON HIS WAY to his room, faculty room 115, he passed rooms 123, 121, doors closed. All faculty doors closed. (Student housing across the courtyard by the pool, all doors open, lotsa loud music.) He passed room 119 seeing the door open.

He had met the couple staying there, they too part of the seminar, but with the lady, he put the scene in Hong Kong. A romance? Unh huh. Eurasian, cool and classy in long skirts showing a little ankle, long sleeved silk blouses and tie strings, open two buttons down, and everywhere she went her husband at her side, yeah, an artist, right there with her, at lectures, teas, parties, he even attended her classes.

Cut it out.

Well maybe not, but just about.

Born for each other.

There you go.

Maybe in love?

You got it.

So, in passing room 119, the gentleman from room 115 looked in, and saw them standing in an embrace, against the far window which overlooked the street, and in the bright afternoon light from off the mountains the features of her face seemed carved, raised up to his, her eyes hot, hungry, wide open. Lips parted, wet, glistening, flat above her teeth: part of his face, cheek, glint of eye gazing down at her, his wavy hair tumbled.

Bam. Kissed her.

Yes?

No. Not right away.

Ha ha ha, oh, no?

No. He lowered his head, a little. She moved yet closer, yearning, panting, neck muscles taut, face up, lips trembling.

Oh!

Yes. Hmmm. Hmm.

In room 119.

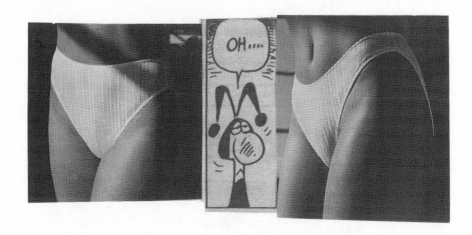

The Big Town

THEY HAD BOUGHT their Venetian blinds on a mail order from Sears, and after getting support brackets in, and blinds installed, their living room looked like a waiting room in a Los Angeles dental clinic, and to their dismay discovered one of the wands — long rods that turned to open and close the blinds — was missing.

So to use them, they twisted the little hook, to which the wand was supposed to be attached, by hand.

The seasons also turned.

Next spring, during a visit to New York, to see Frank and Whatsisname, they visited Macy's where, on the sixth floor, passing through the department that sold curtains and blinds, just for the hell of it Buddy asked the salesman, a black man, if he had a spare wand.

"We bought a set of blinds from Sears," Bang, Buddy's wife said, "and it came missing a wand."

Salesman poker face. "No problem."

"We have to do it by hand." Buddy. Raised his hand, twisting his fingers, showing him.

"Wait here," the salesman said, and turning a large body on small feet, disappeared into a stock room. Door closed.

They waited.

The salesman had had a rather dour expression, as if smelling something unpleasant. Maybe he didn't like his job. Returned though, wand in hand. Gave it to Buddy with a hard, irritated look.

"Thanks," Buddy said.

Bang smiled. Buddy:

"What do we owe you?"

"You bought the blinds here," the salesman said, looking away with sleepy eyes.

Buddy, confused, looked at Bang, a skilled liar. Amazed as she said,

"No." Pause. "Sears." Pause. "We told you."

A ripple of anger crossed the salesman's face, and he said, "Well, in that case you'll have to talk with the manager."

"I'll give you five bucks."

"No no. Speak to the manager." Vague gesture.

They turned, looked behind them, across vast racks of clothes, displays, sales personnel, customers . . .

"Where's the manager?" Buddy asked.

"Over there."

So they thanked him and turning, wand in Buddy's hand, crossed toward and into other retail areas where no managers roamed, and sales people said it wasn't their section for that kind of merchandise, so they kept on walking, right toward the escalator down, and while going down, he said, approaching the fifth floor:

"Why did you tell the truth?"

"I don't know." Pause. "I didn't know what to say. Why didn't you say something?"

"You're a better liar than I am."

Fourth floor.

They looked at each other.

Third floor.

"It's unlike me." Bang.

"That's true."

Both in thought.

"He wanted to give it to us!" she said.

Buddy nodded.

They thought about that.

Second floor.

"What shall we do?"

"Stay off six."

"Want to go back to Frank's?" She laughed.

"Sure."

So hand in hand, they did.

Stepped off onto the main floor which they crossed, passing women's hand and shoulder bags, and perfumes and scarves, precious and not-so-precious gems, toward an Oriental gentleman in formal dress playing an Oriental piano as black as high-gloss German lacquer: *Love Is a Many Splendored Thing*: William Holden on top a high hill, hand in hand with Jennifer Jones whom Buddy called Jump, under a vast blue sky. Thus music, revolving doors and the exit onto 34th Street, where another gentleman, on the corner in the middle of a mob of peddlers and pedestrians, called loud and clear on a bullhorn for Jesus to save us all, why had the salesman wanted to give the wand to them? Nedicks. Hot dog. Onions, relish. Mustard, out. Walking. Walking. That smell! Step step step. A silver jetliner winked in the sun. Windows on the sides of skyscrapers. Yet pigeons almost underfoot. Street vendors. In trash. Beggars. Homeless. Horns honked. Sirens wailed, heavy traffic. Another mystery. The big town.

A Member of The Health Insurance Plan

LARGE, BIG-BONED Grandma, having suffered a sleepless night, dozed at last. Woke unable to breathe and, soon discovered: unable to walk. Phoned granddaughter who called an ambulance. Grandma waited in the lobby, over an hour. Told granddaughter not to bother coming over. Once at her doctor's she'd be okay (whoever knew or knows what that means. She wanted to be alone. Didn't want to bother anybody. Maybe didn't want granddaughter to feel obligated. Maybe granddaughter didn't care. Enjoyed being guilty. Maybe didn't like Grandma. Maybe Granny didn't like her.).

Ambulance arrived. Snap. On a stretcher. Rushed her to The Health Insurance Plan — neighborhood clinic. Black woman, EKG technician, named Helen, recognized her. Found out her doctor's name. Put her in a wheelchair, zipped her around to the office. Outside of which sat a middle-aged white man with dark glasses in a red L. L. Bean jacket, sporting a Jesse Jackson button above the upper righthand pocket. Waiting outside the door. Across a small, narrow corridor. Helen asked him:

"Is this Doctor Friedman's office?"

"Yes." Pointed in front of him. At a closed door. "There."

"Is the doctor in?"

He nodded.

"You can go, Helen," Grandma said. "Thanks a million. You're a dear."

"She's marvelous." The man said.

"Oh!" Helen exclaimed. "Hello!" Recognizing him.

"Hi." He smiled.

"You're so nice." Helen smiled.

He did too.

She had told him last year that her husband had died, two years before. Left her with two teenage children. Boy and a girl. It was tough.

But her son had graduated from high school and found a job he liked, being building super for an apartment house in a plush white neighborhood. She — Helen — was moving to Georgia. Her daughter had finished her first year in college, was away visiting friends.

The door in front of the man with the Jesse Jackson button opened. Doctor stepped out. Saw him. Said:

"Just a minute."

He didn't smile. "Okay."

She reacted to things. He liked that. You could see it happen, in her speech as it crossed her face, Oh, okay, I got it, I get it!

Short, slender, maybe forty. Jewish. Dark, curly hair. Sudden, warm smile.

As a rule he liked and trusted women doctors over guy docs because women were more sensitive. As a rule.

"Well," this woman-doc said, just beginning to say one of those doc-lines, What have we here? did a double-take: gaped. Reacted. Recognized the patient: Mrs. Cohen: Grandma, in the wheelchair, who whispered,

"I can't breathe. I can't walk."

Doc and Helen swapped glances. Doc, to Granny:

"You haven't been taking your water pills?"

Harsh whisper. "No."

Doc. Speechless. Bug-eyed, lips parted,

"You're not taking your WATER pills?"

Gasp: "No."

"But how can that be?" Doc asked Helen, who shrugged. Doc lifted Grandma's skirt, looked at Grandma's ankles.

"The doctor," Grandma began, speaking of another doctor, but this doc interrupted, being a doctor, felt compelled, like dentists, to speak:

66

"What you need is a shot in the arm!"

The seated man smiled.

But as Grandma gripped the arms of the wheelchair, something crossed her face. Gasping for air she raised her head, a wild gargoyle's expression came over her face. Lips stretched. All her teeth showed. Closed her eyes. Body began to shake.

Stethoscope out, pulled up Grandma's shirt, doc poked around. Listening. Spoke, to Helen —

"Give her a shot. I also want a blood test, and an EKG." Pointed look at Helen, who returned the same, spun wheelchair around, pushed Grandma away — Grandma, head back. Face up. Teeth bared. Eyes closed. Body shuddering. The seated man, watching, from behind dark glasses, realized as no one else, that Grandma was laughing.

Two small, agèd, stooped and fragile-seeming Indo-European women in shawls, long, black dresses, materialized in the corridor between the doc and the seated man. One of the ancient women said something the others didn't understand. A large black woman, with an orange scarf over an electric blue dress, handed doc a manila folder, jammed with papers. Which doc riffled. Handed back.

Pointed to another office, "In Room number six. On top of the desk, in the file under 'D.' "

Exit.

"What did you say?" doc asked. The small women. Who repeated their message.

"Oh! That's Doctor Rashid. That way — Room Number Two." She pointed. And the two little ones in black ambled down the corridor, step, by step, by step, step, step, arm in arm, heads down, toward Poland.

Doc shot an index finger at the man in the Bean jacket. Looked through his dark glasses until their eyes met. Cracked:

"You're next!"

Stepped into her office.
Bam.
The door.

Big Family

HE HAD WRITTEN a treatment for a projected screenplay concerning the death of an artist of international fame, and with high hopes showed it to a close friend who wrote for the movies. The friend liked it and sent it off to a movie star he thought should play the lead, meanwhile advising the writer to have a copy of the treatment registered and kept on file at the Writers' Guild of America.

So the writer had a copy made, took the BMT from
Union Square to Seventh Avenue and 57th Street (Carnegie
Hall). Crossed the street on the light, faced west and, on that
light, crossed Seventh Avenue. Kept walking. Noting, to his
horror, that the West End Cafe had closed for renovation!
Meaning in the entire midtown-west part of town there was
only one place to go for a drink, coffee, or a bite, day or night,
before or after concerts: Wine & Apples, because, save the
grimy Irish bars, the rest were Yuppifried.

Well.

No laughing matter, nor food for idle chitchat, because
the Yuppies, having had the city destroyed for them by Mayor
Koch — an uncultured boor — and the real estate circus
masters, New York had become the name of a congested
urban island between Boston and Philadelphia. The avenues
and streets were the same, in name, but the locations were
gone. They used the words "The Village" but there was no
"Village" because there were no bohemians, and everybody
was rich, rents skyhigh, not a bar or restaurant where anybody
involved in the arts hung out. After Max's Kansas City folded,
oh well there were two, three places, Puffy's, Phebe's,
Finelli's — Wine & Apples, but the art world that gave New
York such whopping identity and pride had decentralized.
There was no place except those three places, on that urban
island, to go and hang out with artist pals.

But the Yups thought it was New York because the land
developers had said so. And wasn't that *Central Park*? Wasn't
that *Macy's*? Yes, in name for the young rich, to laze around
the Park, and pad around the gourmet deli in Macy's Cellar.
The homeless poor ringed the Park like a collar, and covered
the sidewalks outside Macy's. The Yups lived in the illusion
created by the developers. Puppets of the puppet-master, they
believed, and continued to destroy the city, to so pollute the
air with their variety of — needless — fourwheeled transporta-
tion, and such mountains of garbage from popular restaurants
and clubs that the homeless poor found food, in sealed

70

garbage bags they ripped open, thus the city became a garbage table open toilet. The Yups of course saw none of this because they were living in *The New York Illusion.* Because they believed, like the ant in Aesop's fable, who put nothing away for winter, against all advice, one day it got cold, he had nothing to eat — one day the illusion will vanish!

Walking west toward Eighth Avenue it was too late. New York just a name on a map. Everywhere he went (he loved to walk), places torn down, he saw by eye, first hand, whole neighborhoods vanish. A bus went by followed by a garbage truck and an ALLIED Moving van. Whipped out his hanky, covered nose and mouth stepping to one side, leaned against a building, closed his eyes, as an ambulance went by the other way, the two paramedics in the front seat laughing as one played with the siren as she might with a clit *screaming.* Or he his. Laughing.

Screaming.

But there was a good breeze. Sky clear, deep Atlantic blue, and in this ugly reality, dreams of writing for the movies. High hopes revived his spirits, crossed Ninth and Tenth Avenues going over the dialogue in the kitchen scene: on the afternoon of the day the artist dies. *He wants to make it with his young mistress, but she won't let him. Her girlfriend had come to visit and is upstairs, asleep. No matter how he begs, his mistress says no. The artist gets angry, and begins to drink.* The task was to make it clear, even at the risk of an overwrite, that if she *had* made it with him, or let him have his way, he might still be alive. So too her girlfriend, who died with the artist, in the accident.

Seeing the giant red 555 he angled across a space like a patio, went through a revolving door and into the lobby, double checked, yep, 12th Floor, turned right, waited for, and entered the elevator, punched 12, and alone, manuscript in hand, rose to that floor, departed for a corridor where he turned left, left again, across to and into the reception area, where he sat on a chair by a small table, under a poster of Jack Nicholson and Meryl Streep in *Ironweed*.

The receptionist a young, good looking fella talking on the telephone.

"Hold on," he said. "Let me see if she's here."

Pause.

"Hi. There's someone named Dan, who wants, okay I'll put him through." Done.

"Did you want to register something?"

"Yes. A treatment for a film."

"Have you been here before?"

"Yes. I know how to do it."

"Good," handing him a manila envelope, with instructions, even so. The writer nodded, smiling. Receptionist did not. Door opened and a gentleman entered in slacks and sport shirt. It was late May, that year, getting warm. The receptionist went through the same exchange with the fellow, who nodded, saying the same as the other writer had, and on receiving his manila envelope, looked at the other. They exchanged looks. Both smiled. Here for the same reason, same ambitions. The writer who had written the treatment felt his heart warm. Became a little giddy, or dizzy, in a fast high, happiness. Began to fill out the questionnaire printed on the face of the envelope. It opened in back, flap on the side, with a large opening rather than the small one on top, with a clasp. This was to be sealed.

The other writer sat near him, small space, and using his manuscript as desk, also filled out his.

Name. Address. Date. Title of Manuscript. Description. Done. Done. Done. Done. *Treatment for Film.*

Looked up, for he had forgotten, so involved with *Ironweed* and being preoccupied anyway, again as always the sight gave him hope, the clout represented gave hope even for his country, perhaps the world. Raised letters, the same white as the wall: *The Writers' Guild of America.*

Took out his checkbook.

"Fifteen dollars," the secretary said, turning and rolling

back to turn again in the swivel chair, to face a typewriter, where he inserted a small letter envelope and typed an address as the writer, both writers, began filling out their checks. Secretary:

"To the Writers' Guild of America *East.*"

Done. Noted on balance page. Torn out, and handed over to the secretary who had rolled forward, took checks as each writer inserted manuscript into envelope and sealed it, passing them over. Good.

The secretary rolled back to his typewriter where he typed out a small form on which was repeated the same as on the face of the envelope, after which he rubber-stamped the registration number in space on the envelope, and on the small form, which he gave to the writer of the film treatment, and began on the form for the other fellow.

Behind, beyond the secretary and across a corridor, a wall of glass and an open glass door, revealed a long room with a *long* conference table and solid-looking chairs, in two of which, women sat, with sandwiches, soft drinks, while beyond them, through a wall of windows, from the 12th Floor, a vista of lower Manhattan, the Hudson and New Jersey. The writer of the treatment smiled. Folded the small form, inserted it in his shirt pocket, just below his Jesse Jackson button.

The other writer accepted his form with its registration number, and turned to leave, met the eyes of the other, and in a brief way, they stood.

"Good luck." Each said. Smiled.

The other departed, but the writer of the treatment hesitated, remembering something he wanted to do, to send a copy off to a writer friend in Canada.

On the secretary's desk, among papers, a legal pad.

"May I have a sheet?"

"Yes."

Humorless fellow, this guy. Yet, perhaps every day, seeing all these big egos, starry-eyed and ambitious come and go, what was amusing? About anything to do, with that? Of course he told his girlfriends that so and so came in today with a new play, to have registered. Oh wow! What's the title, and of course he told them. Don't tell anybody! This stuff is classified! Oh no, never. Never! So yes indeed, nothing much funny about it, not with his ego, maybe he was a writer! Another member of the family. Big family.

On the wall to the right of the secretary's desk, and above, was a framed black & white photo reproduction of four, early-on L. C. Smith typewriters. Crisp. In each typewriter a piece of paper, and on each paper typed, but magnified, easy to read letters in what used to be recognizable as typewriter script.

The writer had a terrific feeling for what was written on those four pages: proud, *very* proud, to be a writer, all the backbiting bickering nasty bitchy bullshit writers involved in swept out over the Atlantic by the brisk late May breeze as he stood, copying each of the four statements. Heart pounding. Realizing how much it meant . . .

> *The stars sell the movie . . .*
> *The director makes the movie . . .*
> *The producer organizes the movie . . .*
> *The writer makes everything possible.*

Walking home, down Ninth Avenue, for just a hint, a whiff of yesteryear, and a touch of the city in Latin crowds, different people, unlike him, thank God: the one slender hope New York had left, and to understand the writer making everything possible was to go out in the world and see it, to be it, to want to be the world by being of it, in it, with and against it no matter how tough, disappointing, frustrating, infuriating for those were the ingredients of making *everything* possible, it never failed, *never,* for him to realize, wherever he was, in the knowledge that he was a writer, and being a writer, he could do it, or come as close as anybody, or anything save God. But — wasn't it? In its genetic structure,

God-given? Wasn't his granddad a writer, and his father? Hadn't his mom wanted to write? She'd written poetry! Remember the classes she took in college? So in that way of walking down Ninth Avenue, he realized it was the writers, not just him, although he would do everything he could, it was the writers together, who could change things, *make everything possible* as he stopped, on 54th Street, waiting for the light to change, looked around him, enjoying all the people, and the broad, busy Avenue.

Because I just registered a treatment for a movie at the Writers' Guild of America—East, I am going to change the world and, by working with other writers, doing it together, we will make everything possible? Am I losing my mind? Writers? *Writers!* WRITERS!! Oh! God *help* us! Writers are EVERYWHERE! THE PLANET IS CRAWLING *with writers*. Ugh. No. *No!* NO! *NO MORE WRITERS!*

Darkskinned people nearby saw a white man in a green sports shirt, with a Jesse Jackson button above his left shirt pocket—shake his head, look up to the sky, and place both hands on his heart. The light changed. Seeming dazed crossed the street with a worried look, to be lost in the crowd.

War

THE SUPERMARKET opened up in the city's newest
renovated neighborhood. Just the thing for young, wealthy
white people, in their expensive clothes filling the aisles.
Waiting in long lines while underpaid black women rang up,
and bagged, their purchases. Never offered a helping white
hand, men in particular. Big guys, watching dark-skinned
ladies heft gallon jugs of Great Bear Spring Water, whole
turkeys, legs of lamb, and six-packs of imported bottled beer:
raise these above the bag, and lower the merchandise down
in while idle, expressionless, pale gray or pink males watched,
in their spirit thick, like wads of money. He liked having black
women serving him. It's her job. She's getting paid. Him in
his 3-piece Paul Stuart suit, silk tie, oxblood leather valise.

And store management, in one more way of cutting back
on labor, used employees who had once been at the cash
registers as floor supervisors (rather than hire mid-
management professionals). It worked, because the employees
were honest. Worked hard. Although at first they thought
the added responsibility meant a raise and perhaps a foothold
on one more rung up the ladder. They were honored, and
proud, until they found they were just plain cheap labor. And
their once bright, eager faces became clouded: angry, bit-
terness verging on sullenness, yet cautious. If they lost this
job they wanted to quit the white man, not be fired by him.
So they continued doing their jobs well, and management
was happy. It expected a large turnover . . . cheaper to let
people go than be involved in promotion. Management was
indifferent, although it could be cruel, vindictive if it wanted,
and this was the American way.

One woman, an employee — floor supervisor — was very good looking, well kept, deep black skin silky smooth, easy to look at. Composed features had an allure that could make a man look twice. Her lips were firm, and touched with red or scarlet, in contrast to her skin, her smile or grin would be something to see, for her teeth were sparkling white. One imagined bright eyes . . . but no, one did not, for her eyes were shadowed, her handsome face a mask, her smile almost a sneer and she never, ever laughed, because she was cheap labor, and she *hated* that job.

She didn't like people, anyway. You could see it. She didn't like anybody. If you had a question, she'd walk right by. She liked that! Smiled — her little sneer of triumph. To black people too! Cold. Nasty, oh so eager to please management. Feared him. White man — or woman. White people. So it was all a trap, made worse by her dislike of people, and inability to deal with people. You could watch as customers, women too, were attracted to her, became repelled, while nothing in her hard, cold face changed. And the all-smiles act she put on before management humiliated her, made her all the more edgy, behind her icy black mask, for she was insecure, frightened and for that held herself in contempt, despising the white man, but wasn't this the American way?

One of her duties as floor supervisor was to also work the information counter where she handled returned merchandise, customer checks, charge sales, answered the telephone, and sold cigarettes, butane lighters, sunglasses, etc.

To her immediate left a small staircase led up to the door to an enclosed office with large smoked-glass windows, where management had a clear view of the floor registers, and the ladies who worked them, as well as of the information counter, right below.

Toward the rear of the store, in an area by itself, was a broad, colorful, very impressive Deli section with an incredible variety of domestic and imported meats, cheeses, pre-cooked and chilled seafoods, custards, and many different kinds of bread and rolls, with baskets of imported and domestic crackers, chips, breadsticks, and prepared sandwich mixes — chicken salad, egg salad, potato salad, tuna salad — herring and sour cream, crabmeat, lobster, and more, all fresh, and tasty and of course everyone in the neighborhood knew where to find all these things, knew what they were, maybe how much they cost, as well as who would be there to serve them, to slice, prepare, wrap, even fill a container of coffee, or tea . . . the takeout at the deli section did a terrific lunch business.

The help in that section, for the most, was indeed helpful, attentive and understanding. In a moneymaking situation where the possible combinations of sandwiches and salads would test diplomats at Geneva: little old ladies unable to make up their mind asking a million questions. Middle-aged minor executives of both sexes in a hurry, but distracted. And — the young and rich who wanted to be pandered to, said okay, a little of that, some of this, quarter pound of that, same of another, with a touch of mayonnaise, Dijon, yes, a couple leaves of lettuce, small dill pickles. Pimento. Black olives? Pitted, please. Holding their printed numbers high for the counterman to see.

But within this busy busyness circled a common attitude, a certain hidden heaviness behind the counter, of contempt for the customer. You knew that produce, vegetables, meat and dairy products sold themselves. The customer took them up front to pay for them. But in the Deli-department, customers had to wait to be served, as they did in the imported cheese and coffee section, and of course for the butcher. But at the Deli counter an air of contempt, behind veiled smiles, became a part of the sale. These employees served their own contempt, and customers, being held in contempt, underwent an experience in humiliation to make a purchase because, or so it seemed, the employees behind the Deli counter hated their jobs because they too were stuck on the ladder. So they hated management. And the customers who made triple what they did. So they hated all of it. This week imported Black Forest ham, on sale—advertised, in all the papers. Customers streamed in to buy the combinations or just the ham itself. But the neighborhood customer knew all too well the purchasing process that lay ahead. With nowhere else to go.

In the middle of the afternoon, one day, a middle-aged white man in dark glasses, a red L. L. Bean jacket (Jesse Jackson above the right pocket), stood at the Deli counter, number in hand, waiting his turn.

Four counterpeople on duty, in their white uniforms making a point to talk among themselves, and on the telephone, at length, animated conversations, thus as if on stage, made the act of slicing half a pound of roast beef a detailed, resentful, grouchy and brooding activity, forcing bugged customers to be patient. They would wait their turn. If not, they could leave. Who the fuck cared?

The employees in the Deli section were both sexes and mixed race, sharing their common attitude. A large black employee with mustache and beard joked with an older Italian employee while customers waited, holding numbers. A small, pale uniform sliced cheese on a machine while a large, full-breasted one down the counter weighed a mix of cottage cheese and peaches.

The man sporting the Jesse Jackson button waited until the black and Italian men laughed and oh ha ha wound down ha ha. The black employee, as if startled, saw the man with the button but looked across at a well-dressed white woman standing a few feet away, and asked,

"Are you next?"

Seeing her number he knew she was not, but the counterman was playing a game. Forcing customers to laugh as if it were a play, to enjoy being humiliated, so the woman laughed, saying she was on her lunch hour and was in a hurry. The black counterman himself laughed, expressed surprise, and looked back at the man with the Jackson button, holding his number.

"You're next?"

"Yes."

The counterman's face changed as if something inward, something blunt, prodded at his brain and hurt him, causing discomfort, and irritation—all this in a wink—his lids lowered, the sides of his mouth curled into a sneer.

"You're *sure*?"

As a big grin split his face. A joke.

"Yes," the other man said. "But she's in a hurry, so serve her."

"Oh," the woman smiled. "Go ahead. There's no real rush."

"But you're on your lunch. I'm not."

The counterman watched with a low smile, yet in a sidelong glance, his eyes darted to the white man. Eyebrows went up.

"Quarter pound Black forest ham." Woman.

While he was slicing the ham, another customer took a number, and waited.

He was a young Latino man, a construction worker on a renovation job around the corner, in worn Levi jacket and jeans. Black sweatshirt over blue shirt, collar out. Worn leather boots. He needed a shave. Dark hair tousled. Long sideburns. Dark eyes. Being patient with the game the counterman was playing.

The young fellow new to the neighborhood, and to this supermarket. More than obvious that facing that landslide of different kinds of breads and rolls, he couldn't make up his mind what to order with the roast beef, for the sandwich which it was clear he was looking forward to.

It was also clear to the counterman who, presiding over the feast of rolls, glowered at the other, and in a nasty tone that could be racist:

"You don't know what bread you want?"

81

"That kind." Pointing to the kaiser rolls. The counter-man took one, sliced in two, and as he sliced roast beef, asked, over his shoulder,

"Anything else?"

The young worker didn't know what to say.

"Whaddya mean?" Soft.

The two men looked at each other. The counterman was much larger, but the worker didn't want to be humiliated. He was tired, and hungry.

"Do you want lettuce, a slice of tomato, mustard or mayo or both, with maybe a pickle?"

"Yeah."

Meeting the worker's eyes, the counterman lowered his, and turned to his task.

A sinister and dangerous game to play, but the counter-man had tested the youth, and lost, which he shrugged off, who cared? Plenty others around.

The man in dark glasses had received his purchase, but waited until he saw the counterman hand the sandwich over to the worker, and again lower his eyes as the smaller man raised his.

And headed toward the front of the store, with the man in the red L. L. Bean jacket not far behind, rather keeping an eye on the youth . . .

But, as by a miracle, one of the checkout registers was open! The express! As though they had waited for him, he breezed right through, yet paused to read on a windowsill the front page of a newspaper concerning Salvadoran death squads murdering native activists in Los Angeles with the FBI looking the other way. Oliver North was quoted — in another column — as saying his mission had failed if the contras didn't get the full support of the American people. During the Congressional Hearings: the Iran/Contra affair. A voice exploded behind him, which cut through the calm buzz of the supermarket like a bomb. The older man turned to see the young worker standing, facing the handsome black

82

woman who had a complicated expression on her face.

They stood by the closed register and loading counter that was closest to the information desk, and management cubicle above. The worker placed the bag containing his sandwich on top of flat, brown bags, between them, and snarled—

"*You* eat it!"

Walked through to the front of the store, yet stopped. Turned. Faced her, he pale with rage, wanted that sandwich, he was *hungry*: "I don't know why you did that to *me,* but *you* go ahead, *you* eat it! It's *yours*"

Walked outside like electricity passing the older man, who kept his gaze on the woman.

Everyeone in the area turned.

The black woman, under the very jaws of management, at the steps up to white power, in her terror of having to pay for the discarded sandwich and afterwards have to eat it herself, or take it home or both, or throw it away . . . it sat there, in its white bag like a lit fuse: burning fast. She didn't know what to do. Didn't know what expression to put on her face, in sweat-popping anxiety she rejected fury, overcame self-conscious embarrassment and placed a smile upon her lips, as if to say oh well, just another creep, yet her eyes were wild, staring at the bag. Her dark face burning, he realized she was fighting not to raise her eyes, to see if management was looking down at her. He saw her fear, her terror, and anxiety. She fought, and fought not to raise her eyes. Her smile as if pasted over a scream, she fought with everything she had just as a customer walked in front of the older man, and blocked his vision which returned in a wink. The black woman had lowered her eyes. She had gained control. And the bag was gone.

He zipped up his jacket and left the store. Walking home he reconstructed it.

The young worker had approached a register, and the black woman had called him over, to check and make sure the Deli-counter man had stapled the cash register tape with the price onto the bag which of course he had. But that wasn't it. She, being powerless—a mere employee—pretended to exercise managerial power in the same war she had learned from the white man. But it wasn't a very rewarding game, as too many black people had discovered the hard way. To imitate the white man exercising power didn't make black people white, it made them frustrated and vulnerable, more victim in a killing rage than ever. But, weren't these games—wasn't this game a war? Wasn't war the nine-to-five? Or, *another* war? Yet wasn't war the American way? Yes. The reason the young, Latino worker exploded, the black woman—faster than the eye of management—snatched that bag from sight.

The Point

THE TWO MEN good pals, enjoyed long conversations on
books, politics, sports, friends, enemies, their jobs, over drinks
in a bar out of town, a roadhouse in fact, yet making sure
the drives back not dangerous, lest wives worry.

The one fellow a criminal lawyer, younger than his
friend, had a violent streak that made certain things he said

stand out long after he said them . . . long even after the lawyer and his wife were divorced, yet they remained friends, something no one would have expected: he went west, she stayed east, and with a nation between them kept contact on the telephone. Apart, together in a new, long distance dialogue.

Before their divorce, however, they had seen the film *The Verdict*. Both had enjoyed it, yet the lawyer's drinking buddy, suspecting they shared what each perhaps wished to avoid in the other, made a point of asking them in separate locations what each had thought of the film, to satisfy his curiosity.

But before he did, in the mere thought of asking, he recalled the scene where Paul Newman enters the lounge of the hotel, sees the woman who has betrayed him, sends her sprawling with a right cross.

It was he thought, odd, to recall this scene, for most vivid to him were the courtroom scenes, in particular the discovery of the new witness. But different people remember different things, he reasoned, yet in himself aware of a difference. So on his next visit with them, in their living room watching the evening news, asked the wife what she thought of *The Verdict*. She like it? She said he liked it. Did *she* like it? Shrugged. Yeh, but he liked it.

"He liked it," she said.

In his study, upstairs, after the lawyer had finished typing a letter. How had he liked it?

"Did you like it?"

The lawyer's eyes blazed. Thin lips split his face. Long, white eyeteeth like fangs as he bared them, cracked:

"YEAH! He *decked* her!"

Not long after the divorce the two friends fell apart, and not long after that the lawyer established telephone contact with his ex-wife. Yet the other never forgot the expression on his old friend's face, with its leer, its fangs, and the words that followed, that rang in the ear, in part because of its

86

obvious character — if he would see a movie like that that's what *he'd* remember, which his pal knew before he had asked, but so had the lawyer's wife, who better than she?

Divorce him! Get him the hell *away* from her, so she could talk to him on the phone. She liked him, she did, but NOT him acting like Paul Newman, which caused a shudder — my God! That look on his face, as he swung!

Doom

WHERE AM I?

Where have I been?

What happened — ?

Heard surf. Smelled brine. Felt sand. On the beach. Oceanside. Overhead starspume, galactic darkness: breathless, infinite freeze frame: the Milky Way.

What happened to me?

Backtracked.

Quarrel with his wife. *"See a doctor for your cold!" "Never!"* Sneezed. Stalked out.

How long was he out here?

Had walked, in long angry strides along the sandy dirt road, toward the beach. *I'm NEVER sick!* Dark, moonless night. *It'll go away!* Off to his left, some ways away, the town of Wellfleet.

Approached a rise in the road. Open area by a pond. Saw a soft blue light intensify. Fade. Felt a wave of drowsiness. Blinked. Found himself in total darkness, sitting on sand, gazing out into space. The ocean. July. In swim shorts, t-shirt. Felt a stab of pain in the back of his leg. Cried out. Hurt his throat. Sore. He, a picture framer: smooth sensitive fingers. Felt leg, in back, right away found the hole. Small, but felt deep. Rose to his feet. Dusted off sand. Headed home. Entered house. Into the living room, where she sat, watching tv. Eating popcorn. Stone-faced.

"Don't think I'm crazy, honey," he said, as if they hadn't quarreled. "Something's happened to me. I don't know what . . ."

"You missed the whole movie. Where were you?"

89

"On the beach. I think. Did I sleep, and dream?" Pause. "Was I gone that long?"

"On the beach? Just great for your cold."

"My throat hurts."

He sighed. Sat beside her on the sofa, had a little popcorn. Coughed. Hurt. Eyes focused on tv screen. The first image, in color, of a boy feeding his dog. In the background, the corner of a white, woodframe house, with a smooth, light green lawn against a deep blue sky formed a composition giving him the distinct impression of being in a large, warm cave, hearing voices he didn't understand.

"What's wrong?" she asked.

"I was inside their ship. Like inside an airplane hangar. In a soft blue light, hearing them talk. But not understanding."

"Ship? What are you talking about?"

"I don't know."

Slumped back against cushions.

To bed.

Woke near dawn. Up, in the bright light in the bathroom, looked closer at the back of his leg. Found the puncture. *Deep.* Near dead faint, caught himself. Edge of the sink. In memoryflash: their fingers, soft as lily petals. Exploring him. Everywhere. Voices, muted vowel combinations, breathing scented with wine. He'd had wine with supper. The air above him, for he had lain on his back, naked, was misty. All darkness beyond. Soft hum, as they explored.

2.

Yet even they, with their advanced technology, they! Masters of the universe!

Or so the promo—word of Empire—went. This trip a low level assignment for sure: investigate and take blood samples from x-number of earthlings. Return home.

Human blood: key to a new, lifesaving vaccine to inoculate their billions on planets throughout the universe. And while returning home, run all samples through the computer, note any irregularities. But as blood dripped from the picture framer's leg, the aliens were having fun again, exploring and playing with him and sipping. These! Skilled, disciplined Hunters! As a strain of something in his blood appeared on the computer screen it went unnoticed. Yet if seen, disregarded. Earthling had a cold. What else was new? Big deal.

Gray, viral blotches like first signs of flu multiplied. Enlarged. Changed from red to white, white cells devoured red rendering the plasma not only impotent, but more vulnerable to the galactic diseases it was supposed to have blocked. A half moon after returning, the crew of the ship and its Hunters, withered. Died. Space ships carried the plasma to all corners of Empire. Subsequent medical discoveries useless . . .

3.

About three years before, he had gone to Boston for a convention. Met a fellow he'd gone to college with, whom he hadn't seen since. Phoned his wife to say he was going to stay over. Couple days.

She heard the laughter and excitement in his voice—she'd heard about the guy.

"Great, honey. See you soon." She had said.

Well, the two pals went on a binge, which, to his surprise (and guilt), included a night with two young ladies, on a fling. They said.

The next morning, hungover, and like the two guys, looked pretty grim. Ladies retired to the motel bathroom, guys popped cold beer. Ladies emerged brighteyed, bushytailed. Laughing. WhhhooooEEEEEEEE! Do it *AGAIN!*

Naked, kissing and licking what guy could resist? And afterwards, wiped out, he noticed needlemarks on her arm, so too her friend's. He said something.

"We're diabetics." She said.

"Should diabetics drink?"

"They should NOT!" Wild laugh. "*I* don't care! Let's have some *fun!*"

"You bet!" cried the other.

Which confused, and depressed him. He felt dreadful. Saying goodbye a relief. In the car going home, drove with care, lest guilt take the wheel.

Pulled into his dirt driveway. Stopped. Out of the car. Into the house. Where she saw. Something wrong. He headed toward his workshop. Normal. There or the beach.

"What's the matter?" She asked.

"He was no fun." He lied.

"Aw. Hey." She said.

Door closed.

4.

On the pretext of seeing a doctor about his cold, he drove to the emergency room of the local hospital. Showed the doc—whom he didn't know—the back of his leg.

Face down on the table, felt the doc probe. Hurt.

"Someone's taken blood." Pause. "Why from the back of your leg? Sit up."

Done.

"That's a deep puncture. There might be an infection, let's take some blood, okay? And do something about that cold. It's summer," the doc smiled. "You don't want to be sick."

"That's true. My wife and I fight about it."

"What's the problem?"

"Doctor, I have never, *ever* been sick!"

"Think it'll just—" snapped fingers, "go away?"

Patient lowered his eyes, yes. Adding:

"I don't want her to know about this."

"Fine. Go down the corridor to room number three. Hopkins will take your blood." Pause. "Come back in a week or so."

Eight days later.

In his office. Doc closed the door.

"Sit down."

Done.

Doc's expression hard, thoughtful, yet sad. Said he didn't know what approach to use to tell him the results of the tests: he'd never had to tell anybody. So, he was flat out going to tell him. And did, handing over a slip of paper with the name, address, phone number of a clinic in Boston.

Patient angry. "I don't believe it."

"Tell your wife." Doc said. "Call the clinic, make an appointment. Don't play with this."

"I'm not homosexual. Nor a drug addict."

Doc sighed.

Patient: "My wife and I are happy. *Very* happy! I have never been unfaith—" Eyes widened. Jaw dropped.

"It's important you tell me." Doc said.

Patient told him. Convention in Boston. College pal. Two young ladies. Not a long story.

But long enough.

"I'll call the clinic." Doc said.

Done: day after tomorrow.

Patient drove home. Followed orders. Told his wife. Boston story. UFO. Bloodletting.

She was thoughtful.

"Well, maybe I've got it, too."

She did.

Evening.

Sitting in lawn chairs. Side by side, in their back yard.

Dark woods near. Ice cubes tinkled. Buzz of insects. From within the house: music. Mozart. *Requiem.* Into the night. She took his hand. He hers. Leaned back. Raised their eyes. Gazed up at the stars.

Death Row and the Open Door

SAID HE HAD HAD recurring nightmares about being on
Death Row: *would* die. No last minute pardons like in the
movies. I wasn't altogether sure why he mentioned it, other
than to relate something of his own to mine regarding prisons,
in light of the novel I was writing, which concerned a job
I had had, teaching in a House of Detention on one of the
Islands.

On the phone I'd mentioned the novel, he said he wanted
the part of the lead . . . well! One of the most famous film
stars in the world. I was flattered. It was arranged we get
together.

He at first nervous, and though I understood — I was the
talent he might want — I was skeptical. He was worth many,
many many millions of dollars, one for each fan, was in excellent health. Clear-eyed. Warm. Vivid. Looked *great,* but
could not open a bottle of imported beer. And almost blushing
called for his front man, a young fellow, handsome by way
of the Sixties, popped the beer, made a wan smile, and turning away, disappeared. I noticed a bottle of Korbel in the
bottom of the fridge — in a small, kitchen area off of the conference room — *Korbel,* I thought. In this superstar layout, 11th
floor of the Warner Communication Building, richest
neighborhood in town.

But if he wanted me to write for him I'd better listen,
and keep details like cheap champagne later, for recall, not
while at his side, walking into the large room with large round
table, heavy, comfortable chairs, windows with a great view
. . . as he sat next to me, or I to him, sipped beer, sure I
didn't want any? I did, but no. I smiled. Thanks.

95

"Actors have to act," he had said, at first. "We *have* to. If we don't, we're fucked up, *more* fucked up, we're *already* fucked up!"

Standing before me, arms out, he laughed, I did too — what he said was true — like what he wasn't saying, also true. More true. If he *had* to act, he HAD to have writers. Without writers there would be no movies. No television. No media. No culture. Civilization. World.

It was not lost on me that I was one more on a string of writers he had interviewed, and that my novel had little chance to be taken for a film starring him, yet on the other hand, this was an unusual day in the life of a writer, and I would be as conscious as possible, not to talk talk talk on the many ideas I'd had, on my own, regarding movies.

So I listened.

And, if it is possible, liked him. Wished I could know him better, if that can ever be. He went to lunch with a famous director, leaving me at the table, to think my thoughts, go over my notes on things we'd discussed, and await his return. But he didn't return. A secretary asked that I leave copies of my outlines and, with a sad, professional expression, said he was flying down to L.A. in the morning. They'd be in touch with me.

That was that.

But even so, even though nothing came of it, I yet see him there before me, just as seen in his several smash hits, the illusion he created was amazing. Being so relaxed, not just like "one of the guys," but above, at ease, cool in a high place, one of the gods. A creative one, at the moment interested in me, meaning every detail stood out: his casual, expensive light blue, vee-necked sweater, tan slacks, with the narrow leather belt, just that touch, the new, "in" look of the Fifties, *nothing* personal, save perhaps the generosity of his illusion. With his every glance away I looked closer, indeed he knew I would, his every aspect flawless, in particular the way his tan, his almost impeccable light tan, muscular body

96

moved, beneath the clothes, under his direct, clear eyes and beautiful fingers, reaching for the bottle of beer, I had a feeling of the fall of Rome.

In retrospect he was brave: with all the money and fame anyone would want, he yet needed another talent: a writer. Writers. *Actors have to act.* He'd complimented me — he'd read some of my books — saying he enjoyed my dialogue, and the man/woman thing. His words: "The man/woman thing."

But he knew that every move he made, every gesture, every look, had to appear in his context, to draw me in in the specialized way he needed, and wanted, because it had to work. First and last it *had* to work. And this little interview, with his front man, secretaries, and advisors in the wings, perhaps even listening, this little stage play was his high point of vulnerability, the true place in Fate's script where he would reveal himself. So he had to rig it, lest the revelation be grotesque. Tense scene: the puppet approaching his puppet master.

In fear of saying the wrong word I almost bit my tongue.

"I want to be in good movies," he said. "That's all I want."

"I think you ought to direct," I said.

He bent his knee, propped up his foot and began untying the shoe, soon changing into sneakers, and as he laced up, looked at me.

"Oh yeah?"

Smiled. Eyes twinkling.

Did my heart flutter?

But the reason he changed shoes, like people who quit smoking, he didn't know what to do with his hands, he used his hands a lot in his films, of course, the sneakers for walking, to the restaurant for lunch. But his hands were so fast, they untied and tied laces with incredible precision.

"Unh huh," I replied. "I have an outline here, based on a story by Robert Louis Stevenson. There are three characters. Two of whom are aspects of the protagonist's personality

—he's a divided man. The third is the man he kills. I've written it with you in mind, to play the three parts, and to direct it. For a one hour Christmas special, on Educational Television. It takes place on Christmas Eve."

"Let me see it."

I leafed through, found and handed it on. He glanced at it, saying it looked good.

"I'd like to do stuff for tv."

"You'd be great."

"Yeah?" Sparkle. "Think so?"

"People love you, they'd have you right there, in the living room. Live." I smiled.

He did too.

We talked about that for a while, as I had several ideas, and he seemed pleased. But of course his people, his script readers, would determine everything. I didn't stand a chance. This was just fun.

Him saying yes until they said no.

"How'd you get involved with prisons?"

"Through a friend who taught there," I said. "He'd gone on vacation, had a chance to go overseas. I filled in."

We looked at each other.

"I liked it. Lots of talent behind bars, so," with a shrug, "I continued."

He nodded, we talked about that, and it was hard not to believe he wasn't interested, or at least thoughtful, but then he's won an Oscar, and wasn't going to stop acting because I was there, so aware he was such an interesting, and interested, nice, good guy I a little lost touch with myself, the illusion was so real, he was a good even great actor it seemed unfair to believe this was his stage. His theater. He confided in me—

Said he wished the director he was having lunch with would let other writers write for him, and not *always* write his own stuff.

"Yes," I agreed. "I heard that."

Received an inquisitive look.

"I heard he writes all his own material," I said.

"Oh. Okay," he said.

What had he thought I had meant? Maybe he didn't know, did he want me to tell him?

You're insecure, I thought.

You're right, he did not say.

I think he hated these interviews. I think he *despised* them in an absolute *hatred*: they take him away from his personal self and those devouring wants the *way* he wants, he had, he HAD to relate, be persuasive to the one person and talent — in the whole world — who in reality frightened, made him insecure, even TERRIFIED him. This was the most hated part of the whole movie process, but you bet, one he acted through so well — the corporation sure was his! — if *he* needed a writer, *he'd* talk with that person. Good. I admired him, or as I was admiring him he blurted.

"I have recurring dreams about being on Death Row." Paused. "Not so much anymore."

"Hm!" I exclaimed. "Why?"

"I mean," I hastened to say, "why would you have that dream?"

"I don't know," he answered, and after a pause, confessed: "I was in therapy."

"Me too. Off and on for fifteen years."

He murmured something about not having been in that long, and he didn't like that although he didn't say so, a sort of cloud crossed his face. I said,

"It sounds like guilt."

Let that sink in.

"Why would you be guilty?"

A look came over his face the way moisture appears in balloons, his lips parted to say *I don't know* except that he did know, but wasn't telling. The games actors play with themselves are not simplistic or superficial: if he or she comes alive in front of a camera, a lot of things happen at once that go everywhich way. One of those things is fame, and with him an early, explosive overnight, worldwide fame which affected every aspect of his personality, beyond his wildest, most ambitious dreams . . . With Death Row incubating anyway, in various corners since childhood: nothing less than death awaited him, in his much more than mere, idle interest in prisons: places where people go to be punished. *Death.* The Electric Chair. By The Neck Until Dead. Or The Guillotine — name it, right there on the Row, waiting. Over and over and over, recurring.

But my question, Why would he be guilty? after saying it sounded like guilt, I think threw him. Being unable to say anything that made sense, he switched tracks — well, he's no longer on Death Row, why should he answer me? And besides, he had to bring the scene back to him. Things had gone out of focus! Puppet master had asked a question puppet couldn't answer, so he stepped to one side, ignored it, and said long ago he had had a passionate desire to not just be in prison, but be on the Yard, with the inmates, you know, to be out there, so through a priest he got in, disguised in dark glasses, black watchcap and I think a mustache, among prison inmates this superstar, around the end of the Sixties, was walking around the Yard at San Quentin. Terrified, he said, yet excited. Tended to keep to himself, stayed near the walls. Insisted he just wanted to know what it was like. To be there. See for himself. Well, a guard spotted him skulking about, and not recognizing this inmate, walked over to him, told him to go up against the wall — eyes blazing, he showed me — arms up, legs spread — the guard frisked him and found a tape recorder! Jumped back, yelling at him, *Where'd ya get this?* In real terror, actor *petrified!* Ripped off his watchcap, dark glasses, mustache, screaming The Graduate! *The Graduate!* Shrieked, THE GRADUATE! until, dumbfounded, the guard recognized him.

"You're — you're —" pointing at him.

"Yes! YES! YES! Lemme *out* of here!"

100

Confusion!
Craziness!
They let him go.

The next day, he did fly down to L.A., and I haven't seen him again. His people did not return my notes or outlines, nor the many calls I made, until several weeks later, out of the blue, the woman who had told me he would not be back from lunch, phoned to say my material had been rejected by their first reader, but I should feel free to approach them with anything I felt they might use. The door was open.

The Last Real Artist

THE MEETING was OVER! *Great!*

Shook hands with smiles with President Bello, and in the company of other executives turned, crossed toward the door to the conference room, in corridor outside waited for and caught the capsule floating down feeling no descent, to emerge with the others in stride to their private Veels, hovering above the green of the Mall, door clicked shut said hi to the pilot, the small ship in an upward slip moved as still as air towards the mountains, very fast it flew, crossing the city on an angle beyond: Misty, his ranch came into view.

Down.

Out.

"Thank you!"

"Nice weekend, sir!" Pilot smiled.

"You too," forgetting the guy's number. Stepped off the landing platform onto his front lawn which he crossed, through the front door cavity on spoken code, across the living room floor, not seeing its details — the very latest in Twenty-Second Century living — toward the rear of the house. His wife not home, down south on a dig. A freak earthquake in Southern California had revealed three houses in excellent condition, just as all their contents — according to found newspapers (printed on *paper!*), from the mid–Nineteen-Nineties which included a red Baby Honda in the garage, in mint condition, you want to talk about treasure, there it was!

Strode into his bedroom, kicked off cowboy boots — scuffed from acrylic stacks in storage, sat on his — (their) bed, and unclasping garters, peeled off black silk stockings.

Wiggled aching toes.

Stood up, flung jacket onto bed, undid bow tie, red diamonds on black pattern, hand tied — tossed away, pants down, off onto the bed, too or, more proper, their orange, black, blue and green floral patterned eiderdown. Unbuttoned shirt, removed cufflinks, gold with ruby settings, taking no care to be neat. Quite the opposite. Home at last, to hell with it. Ran his manicured fingers through styled, light gray wavy hair combed to one side, with a part he messed up. Nice looking guy taking off his underpants. Naked, smiling, stood on wall-to-wall carpeting, thick, light blue shag, framed by beige plastic walls, room featuring muted natural wood and white furniture in style a cross between Stockholm and Taos, X-penseef. (*Natural* wood, not that cheap moon-mica junk. The work of the little lady? Don't you believe it. It came with the house.)

Eager, naked, barefoot feeling *I got nuthin' on and I am free,* brisk walk, strode out into and along a corridor leading (on an angle away from the garage and their personal stables) to his studio, the door of which he unlocked, pushed open, and entered in a sensory rush as happy as a boy on the first day of summer: a sensory smell of paint, turpentine, linseed. Closed door, bolt. Click.

Alone!

Worn wooden director's chairs with different colored canvas slings (how he got *those!* Good story), placed here and there, with dirty clothes in piles beside them or draped over, clothes on the floor as well, scattered around before the easel which stood — on moveable base — some twenty feet away, facing a director's chair with a small table beside it, with a small plate, half-finished sandwich and empty glass of milk. The painted image on the canvas appeared unfinished.

Many other canvases, large and small — all stretched — finished and not, leaned against walls. Some quite large . . .

Spacious louvered windows (open) gave a view onto just the edge of the rear of the garage, and the back yard which, aside from his neighbor's vineyards, off a mile or so to the north, looked out toward the pale green foothills, some thirty miles away, half hidden in trails of mist. Cattle grazed in the foreground. Cowboys on horses . . . under a big sky as far as, farther than the eye could see. Nobody could see that far, the sky went up up and up, out of sight, way out, up there and all blue. The humidifier creating *that* illusion cost one fuckin' *fortune.*

Seeing none of this the man picked through clothes around the floor, putting on faded jeans splattered with white paint, pair of old, thick blue socks, white with a broad red band around the top that used to be called *boot socks,* tugged on and feet shoved into battered, paint splashed, ankle high leather boots, leather thongs which he laced, humming as he tied 'em up but not too tight — they had looked loose in the movie . . . kept 'em loose. Got into a wrinkled, smelly, paint spotted red and green, blue chambray shirt which he tucked in, and although he didn't smoke, he lit up an airfilter and, pretending to inhale all that a cigarette had once been, crossed to the chair by the small table and flipped on a small, microwave hotplate. Soon he sipped from a small enamelled cup, a strong, thick black liquid that was once Turkish coffee and would yet be, but for the Firewars.

If anyone asked him, however, he'd reply,

"I drink coffee: black." Real artists drank *coffee.*

Day and night.

Sipping, he looked round the room at the paintings, including the one on the easel, which he had quit working on couple of days ago because he ran out of which artist it was he had been as he painted, and couldn't get back into character — what he imagined — until he wanted to with a passion, for that was it. To be one of them and paint! They were the real ones! So few books had been written, so few films completed, there was so little information that if you wanted to be DeKooning, and paint, what, and who were you? What did — what do you think, *what are your thoughts* if you are DeKooning, and facing the canvas on your paint wall, how do you think DeKooning's thoughts while you paint while dressed like him, or dressed like Al Leslie? Or Franz Kline.

105

Jackson Pollock! How did they, what did they think? He had studied the paintings from that period at great length, and he thought that if Al Leslie painted like Franz Kline, like Mike Goldberg and Milton Resnick had DeKooning, and George Spaventa, Giacometti! If he imitated, and dressed like Al Leslie, or Franz Kline, and noticed the big gesture Al Leslie took from Franz Kline, he could copy what Al Leslie saw, but what did Al Leslie think? Why hadn't anybody written it down? There were no clues, until he discovered the clues were in the paintings, that they were trying to get away from thinking the kind of thoughts someone could write down, and instead get lost in what they were doing, so they bought the clothes they wore because the clothes were cheap and sold in nearby stores under the Third Avenue El, but that did not convince him because he was certain if for example he dressed like Jackson Pollock according to the photographs by Hans Namuth, no matter where they bought their clothes if he wore them and walked on large sheets of canvas like Pollock had in those photos, and threw paint and dripped paint on the canvas like Pollock his boots too would become splattered, so would his Al Leslie jeans, his DeKooning's blue chambray shirt, even the wristwatch on his left wrist the kind Franz Kline wore, with black strap, grateful for that detail! —they never wore hats in their studios. Neither did he. Their hair became touched by paint, so did his. Nor did they—nor he! —wear eyeglasses although he had to, in reading.

But it infuriated him that he could not be Marisol and *nobody* understood, always talking about sex, her work got him into wooden figurative sculpture that made him happy, and, he discovered, she too dressed in jeans and chambray shirts, so did Joan Mitchell—Motherwell too! *This mode of dressing had true meaning, but what was it?* In the days while sculpting what Marisol had, he discovered what she wore, had some of them done it like this? Dressed like that and then painted? Joan Mitchell in France! Even there! In those clothes . . .

106

Yet their art was so different from each other's, but so were they! And they dressed the same, once, it was true, Easter Island had been a mystery, but this, different men and women doing different work while appearing the same, how else could you paint like them, but wear the same clothes, maybe close your eyes, and trying to think why the women in DeKooning's paintings had those big eyes looking nothing like the photos of Marilyn Monroe's eyes but DeKooning said in his titles it was her. DeKooning was one of the *most* real artists, for he was deep.

All this of course done and thought in secret, in his secret studio. Who would understand? Or care? That as he began a painting wearing those clothes and thinking, he thought, like whoever it was he intended, and in the process began what to him looked like another maybe Gorky he began he thought to think like Rothko, his painting on the easel or paint wall changed, the Franz Kline artifacts, the German cigarette lighters! what emerged were painted works that to him looked so original he couldn't imagine anyone having done them, anyone *he* could imagine. He framed the good ones, put 'em on his living room wall, along with 22nd Century life styles, prrrreeeeety weird.

"Who did those?" people asked.

"God knows," he replied. "Came with the house."

"Worth anything?"

"Plenty."

"Are they signed?"

"On back."

Wife and close friends thought he was crazy, in the language of future days. But, so what? Who cared? Hadn't they thought those things about the *real* artists? That obscure magazine calling Jackson Pollock "Jack the dripper" . . . so, he was, therefore, very happy, couldn't wait to get home after work, Thursdays best of all, with the weekend ahead. He did dozens of paintings, and every one looked to him at least like a work in paint, real pigment, maybe a little maybe a lot like one of those masters from the distant past, in the middle of the 20th Century that he *knew* were the real ones, the modern ones who used paint, not technology, and they had paint on their clothes, and hands, in union with the paint on the canvas: they dressed in what they were doing in paint.

He'd almost wept having read somewhere that the tar on streets, that paint that had spilled on sidewalks, that small town/big city junkyards, auto wrecks, soup cans, skyscrapers, oceanliners, tugboats, construction sites, people screaming, were the essential identity, organic substance, and secret code for the painting of that period . . . *art had been everywhere.*

And his discovery that all those artists knew each other, lived and painted in *one* neighborhood, and went from their studios out to *just one* bar dressed in the same clothes they painted in, and drank and maybe got drunk and were *not* arrested — or shot! all made him dizzy, his head spun, sending him into such happiness he — in all honesty had to rest. The Vice President of Chemtelray Plastics, Beef Scent Ltd., facing a half-finished canvas, dressed in the same clothes his heroes wore, paint brush in hand, their faces and figures flashed through his memory — who, today? *Who?* Tantalized him, *made him so happy . . .*

Out on the illusion of plains and mountains, colorful android cowboys on movielike android horses gazed into eternity, while seeming to move, remain fixed, under the deception of a deep blue sky, in an icy cold night void stretching out beyond the end, toward and into nothing, vast and dreamless.

Far Out

DUSTIN HOFFMAN had called him up, and after praising his writing, arranged they get together, which they did, in Hoffman's corporate office, high in the Warner Communications Building. Great view. And after talking a while about a job the actor wanted the writer to do — read a couple of scripts and make evaluations — Murray Schisgal, Dustin's chief advisor came into the room, smiled hiya, shook hands, sat near the actor and after this and that Dustin asked the writer had he seen any movies?

Thought a moment. "Winkler."

"I haven't seen it."

Murray shook his head. Shrugged.

"A West Box film," the writer explained.

Dustin, who looked plain out wonderful, healthy skin color, in shape all around, yet frowned —

"West Box?"

Murray didn't say anything. Dustin had turned, a little, and looked at him.

The writer named several films Box had directed.

"Ohhh," the actor murmured. "Ohhhh, yeeeaaahhh . . ."

"My best friend wrote the screenplay."

Hoffman's eyebrows went up. Asked,

"You know him?"

"Sure."

Crossing the actor's face like the music in *The Day the Earth Stood Still.*

"How is he?"

"Okay. Good . . ."

Sleepy-eyed. "Yeah?"

"Yeah!"

"What's he doing? Working on anything?"

And a voice as clear as the cry of an owl at midnight *spoke into the writer's ear and said:*

"Sh."

"He's out of town."

Anybody who knew him knew he was out of town, was always out of town, even if he *was* in town, was out — on his way, out.

Next day he called him — he was in town, and said let's have lunch. He mentioned Dustin, and Murray.

So they did. On Third Avenue.

He told him what had happened, which he thought was funny. The other fellow, defensive, thought it was pretty wild. Didn't he? Sure. And just before he told him, you know, about what the owl had said, the pro scriptwriter said,

"That's the hook. That's how they work. They want you, so Dustin hangs his hook outside your window with your name on it, and gets you." Pause. "He'll say yes until he says no."

"Murray will."

"Right. Murray will, and he *will* say no." Pause. "Don't talk too much about me."

Okay.

They ate lunch.

"But I don't understand," he said to his best friend, "where, how did all this — "

"After *Tootsie* I went to Japan with him." His dimples are deep as he laughs, and he laughed at the funny expression on the face across the table: a Buddhist sense of humor.

"But — "

"He wanted to do a remake of *The Treasure of Sierra Madre,* and wanted me to write it."

"But you wouldn't."

"Yeah," with a sigh, his friend watching him remember

110

working for the big studios on the big smash hits, becoming sicker and sicker, the total masochist . . .

"I couldn't do it," he confessed. "He offered me a hundred thousand." Pause. "A hundred thousand."

"And you said no."

Another reason they were friends.

"That's right," he said. "I couldn't do it. Not again. So I said no." Pause. "I never went back to Hollywood . . ."

"Bet he was pissed off." Pause. "Bet he was." Smile.

The other smiled, too. But it faded. He looked out the front window of the restaurant, and didn't say anything.

Her Royal

ON THE SECOND DAY of the new year, 1940, in a town in Vermont, a small boy sat at his mother's new Royal portable typewriter, and (having in secret watched her), rolled in a clean sheet of paper, and wrote the first words in his long, distinguished, mother-dominated literary career:

hello my bame bane name is lie   lela land sorter sna i li liv live at

"You silly boy," she interrupted, "no no NO!" in laughter, even singing, as she danced into the room, hands conducting — and, propping him up with a cushion, getting him comfortable, said,

"Push the shift button down, and the letter you want capitalized, like *this*!"

And zippety zip, did a rewrite. Signed both their names and dated it, which in his middle years, was recalled in a session in therapy, that the color of the new car he'd gotten his wife for a Christmas present was darker than a royal midnight . . .

The therapist's deadpan expression, as in a mystery, made a subtle change.

"Yes?" she asked.

Forseeing the abyss he had created in that slip — the significance of a new car for his wife, and the color of the car matched — he realized — the color of his mother's Royal typewriter, he did what every good patient does: admitted the slip, told the history of the typewriter and, realizing aspects of his wife reminded him of his mother, in an unhappy honesty crossed a new threshold in therapy, which lasted many

many moons. But, at a certain point, in a giddy (illusion of) clearness, after a session he joked,

"They don't make word-processors that black," big grin.

Royal midnight, thought the doctor. *They?* But being civil, letting a little sparkle into her eyes, smiled,

"No, they don't. See you next week."

"Good," he replied, stepping out into the Boston night, but not five steps away wondered maybe the doctor didn't like him, and with that very notion realized she had dark eyes, black as—

Causing a little obsession, which the good patient decided to follow through on . . .

"Well," the doctor said, "you're touching all the nerve ends at once. She's showing up everywhere, even in my eyes. Why don't you write about it?"

"How?"

"I don't know. You're the writer." Come *on.*

"I'll think about it . . ." obvious dismay.

"Why don't you write a poem? You see her everywhere . . ." Doc smiled. *Do* it!

The patient laughed, wondering why the doc had smiled, and so it went, cause for at least a novella, or a full fledged novel—many novels, one for every man, woman and mother, until the end of the world.

*   *   *

Near dawn of the third day of the New Year, 1940, in that small town in Vermont, little Leland's father, having heard about mom making the discovery of Lee at her new Royal, tiptoed into her study, and having had a fight with her, that Katherine Anne was *not* Katherine Anne Porter's real name, in a sullen, bitchy and deceptive way he had, Leland's father looked deep into the tall bottle of Bellow's Partner's Choice, which with a glass of ice and small bottle of club soda, looked back at him until everybody else was fast asleep,

114

and he had the courage to sneak into her study, snap on the light, and on the same sheet of paper Lee — and she — had used — still in the typewriter — he wrote with difficulty, in single space, the following:

The tall green and yellow ringed glass filled with whiskey and soda, stands on a round cork coaster, on white oilcloth, in a smelll of cinne cinn cina cimma cinamon toast

One woman was unwilling to be govene governed by two, as in air travel, people accepted and settled into the job the other woman offered her, which in hatred without speech to her boss, she kept, although in silent faith, Katherine Anne Porter's faith which turned out was a lie, therefore while in faith and fact kept, she kept continuing with the man, the same man, with perhaps mp more fact than faith, to whom the boss had turned for a glimpse through his lens, into her soul, while her husband had for, had made, for downhome fact made with she whom had sought the job, and was hired, which explains why — was why, although np not before he who possessed the lends lens adored a woman across an eva ever remarkable — by its depth — body of water while she on — the other side — across that body busy with her lens, kept pace with her work and face up, eyes closed, lips parted on his occasional visits to her, her visits to him, to flirt with, this lens business tricky insofar as what gets said and who believes it, seeing not what is said, hearing from whom to who, and in this way explains the msytery of her pregnancy, and subsequent discovery of the mistaken father, as seen by the man with the lens, observing the creature under his glass — not she over the body! Nay! But she who shall stay! — not to be governed by any even as in air rtravel yea, not to mention the who woman that loved her, because she didn't want to be loved, but poz possessed by the man with the lens, who in his convex heart and concave soul knew that the woman who hired the woman who hated her ala the author Porter was the woman he loved, and wanted, but feared, because she had no lens, and beckoned in that way beyond air yravel travel — iced tea and connamon cinnemon toast to baffle us all — or almost, almost all, because some of us, for faith, fall neither for love nor fact, and on the fateful journeys always involving departurem toward sure or unsure

115

*destinations, IN ALL SEASONS. In every change: demand the face
we will know, involving neither she, nor him, but white oilcloth and
mine.*

*   *   *

Two days after Thanksgiving, 1993, Leland's mother
died. She was very old, very tired, and ill and as everybody
knew, in truth it was a blessing, but Leland — the only child —
in the usual aftermath, had to go through all her papers, deal
with the lawyers and take care of the house — and housekeeper
who had become a friend. It was a lot of work, and took him
away from his new novel, but it had to be done. So.

He hadn't known of her past interest in poetry and the
arts and was somewhat astonished, to go through her books
to find small anthologies and literary magazines, that had
published work of hers! She had spoken of a talented aunty
Nan, but . . . to his amazement, on opening a Random
House anthology of poems by poets under forty he found her
listed, with *six* poems! And on the bio page, there she was,
in the best of the up and coming . . . yet, which caught his
eye, as he hadn't looked, did a doubletake, it had been edited
by his father! And in the back, pasted in among good reviews
over the endpapers, his, Leland's own first effort that day on
his mother's Royal, followed by her rewrite *and* dad's . . . he
sat, crosslegged on the floor in her bedroom, surrounded by
boxes, papers, books, magazines . . . stunned, he read it
again, scalp tingling. Raised his eyes, glanced across the
room, saw the case, it had to be. Upended on the floor, between her dresser and her bookcase. Got to his feet, strode
across, lifted it up, and dusting it off, placed it on her bed,
where he opened it: the typewriter his father had gotten for
her in 1940, so she could continue to write poetry and, maybe
in the fun of it, he, her editor . . . Leland's eyes misted, gazing down on the quiet, gleaming black machine, with its

116

mysterious scent of oil, the magic in her fingertips, her hidden labyrinth of poetry . . .

And so he learned some things in life were not to be communicated. Save through language used in that way—
". . . *In every change: demand the face we will know, involving neither her, nor him, but white oilcloth and mine.*"

You see? *Who* could ever understand, in the emptiness after his father's death, and all his father's games of deception meaning there had been another man to her and a woman to him but in the end neither, but a clean white surface, in a poetic hint of his reflection, as his secret focus. His anchor. His perfect trust.

And of the son's once up-and-coming mother poet? Who had given it to him, all too much so, yet to nourish and encourage and at every turn to show her pride in him, he was so special—yes!

She his, and meant to be. Therapy had given him that—and a lot more. He understood, and—in that neat, controlled, *good* man he was, no one would know what happened as his hands opened the case, to her—to that typewriter. All this had been difficult on his wife, and their children. Leland's subjective period with his dying mother, and on planes going home and coming back, a trying experience for all. Well.

On New Year's Eve that year, his wife and their kids, the boys and their sister, saw him to their astonishment fill a tumbler a third full of whiskey, add ice and club soda, and say, in measured tones to a writer, a novelist friend that Katherine Anne Porter was *not* her name, she was poor white trash from Texas and—

"Yes," the other fellow said. "That's true. Funny, isn't it?"

Leland gave him a dirty look and said,

"Yes, that is funny. But you will never understand, and I don't think I will either, but *there is something there.*" He then apologized.

Turned to his family. The same.

Everybody smiled.

But he had another whiskey, with club soda, and though pleasant and all, people who knew him knew he was not himself.

After everybody left he stayed up. Insisted on it.

"Aren't you coming? It's *two*."

"I'll be there. Shush!"

Near dawn he went into his study, took the colorless word-processor away . . . picked up his mom's Royal from the corner, and put it on the desk. Turned on the desk light. Opened it, and with his drink beside the machine, rolled in a sheet of typewriter paper and sat, looking. Had a sip. Closed his eyes. Rubbed his forehead.

Sat back.

She gave her gift to me, he thought. And saw his mother, and — there! — his father, both, looking at each other, in silence, and in a way, in their way, turning to look over their shoulders, saw him, so he leaned forward, in the faint, sweet, machine oil scent, and full sight of the gleaming, smooth black Rolls-Royce shape, held his hands above the round, silver-rimmed keys, and where none but her fingers had been save once by his as a boy, and his father's the next day, he touched the mystery of her memory:

Again

She didn't dream what she dared she'd believe: never believing what she would dare to dream. She wanted him to tell her. He wanted her to dare.

118

The Woman in Red. The Frog in the Emerald Valley. The Dawn. The Birds. The Veil and the Thirty Days.
Celery Stalks at Midnight.

for Celina Herzman

RALPH WAS A FOOL and in part knew it, buying another gift for his wife, one more present—what could she give to him? Who always gave? Neither in truth understood because they were young, too involved in living life to come to conclusions about it. That he had a problem taking things, which in fact meant *her*—do you think she knew?

Hmm. Hmmm.

Say yes.

So the two reasons she went into the arms of the other man, who was older (and married with kids), was because she thought *he* would see her as she wanted: beautiful, young, and individual, yearning to be taken, for she was weary of being nice, and in secret wanted to rip loose.

This — wouldn't you know — as she and Ralph had each begun therapy, so it was in that way that he had an awareness, coming as it does in the first weeks of betrayal, in small, intuitive ripples, and he (like her), in that game of hide and seek was not yet clear how conscious he was of her, knowing she was indifferent to sex with Ralph, yet wanting him to see her as she was (but he didn't, which was why, after they got back together before Jimmy Carter was elected, she divorced him). Yet she feared to be taken, in screaming, panting release, and losing her controlled, composed, too aware but beautiful self even seen as object which she cultivated, as she did with beautiful things, of substance. Ceramic vases, figurines, etc.

She talked a lot — a *lot* — to Ralph about her father, who had come up, she said, in therapy. Ralph realized she looked like her dad, had his eyes and eyebrows. She told Ralph that during the first session, right away, *bam,* her therapist had gotten her to talk about her father, but not saying why.

So Ralph gave her a present, because he was always giving, because he wanted things smooth, and because he was a fool. She too. Yes. Her secret lover didn't want to take her into convulsive ecstasy, he wanted to fuck her because she was beautiful and wanted to be in his arms, he thought, and make her happy in his way, not hers, which she realized right away, but not knowing what to do, for she was young and stupid, she allowed him to have his way, which meant he made himself happy, using her and she in his way by obeying his instructions, in their secret *liaisons not* wondering what, in reality, was going on. That's where she was unfair. The infidelity wasn't working, was kind of grubby, even embarrassing. She didn't question any of it, but allowed it to go on, and on, and feeling oh a little guilt because of Ralph that dummy yes that dummy, who loved and without question trusted her and, she knew, if he found out he'd understand. He'd hope she was happy. He'd think he'd failed her. But she didn't ask why, for she was *very* involved in her self.

Sex with Ralph at home or on trips was good or not or okay, he often came too soon and she would never say a word, men so sensitive about it, nor did he speak, in fear of the forbidden (she might agree), but a man knows, and he did stay with her until she came, too, and he was glad, and happy, but in secret angry because in the way it was, the way she was, taking so long to get in bed while he waited there, he almost realized it wasn't him, but because he didn't question her, why should he? over who it was, or for that matter was not, he was sure it wasn't another man she dreamed of, as she came, but it wasn't Ralph, either, and that was clear, and there he let the matter rest. Who, he didn't wonder, was it?

It had to be an illusion.

He didn't like her father and her father didn't like him. So after visits with her parents which he hated, watching her sleepwalking father come on to her, in those tender little papa strokes and touches, as daddy looked at her Jesus your skin would crawl, so he bought her the newest paper edition of their favorite mystery writer, whose books they enjoyed discussing (plot, characters), and she said,

"You're giving me something you want. Why don't you buy something *I* want?"

"I thought we'd both like it." Apologized.

She looked at him, a low gaze turning her beauty into a mask, making her seductive. It took some living to realize what she wanted, and that in the distant future it would become a mask of understanding, as that of a professional social worker's, which not even the most wonderful man can talk though. But that came later, after the divorce . . . she had returned from overseas and her new husband to visit her parents, telephoning Ralph to make a date, in the Park, which depressed him, but he met her.

She said she was glad to see him, that she had thought of him, and . . . oh but he knew it was over, *long* gone, because, he saw, she had become much less interesting, less alive, less tempting, and he wondered what it would take to see her in her European life: in her mask of understanding it occurred to him that he was an irrelevant, but established memory. It felt so strange, to see himself disappear, *poof!* in her. What once was right here is before your eyes gone. He did not want to see her behind her mask because — rattling him — the mask was real.

He had kissed her on the cheek, sat beside her on a bench in the sunshine. They talked.

Weird.

But like men who think they come too soon, and do, he wanted to fuck her again in the dream it would be better. Such men abound.

How can you think of such a thing? she would ask, in disgust. Or, Is that all you can say? Or, Is that *all* you think of, on seeing me? Or, Can't you think of *me*? Can't you — you mean, *still*? *That's* all you want?

You go right home and tell your husband, maybe he'll fly over and kick shit out of me. He could have said.

But, meanwhile, back in the youthful days of their marriage, what was left of it, and afraid to do what he *knew* she wanted him to: see her as she wanted him to, he knew he wouldn't like what he saw (not what she meant), although he wanted to, so he gave her a present. Another book of crossword puzzles.

Ha ha!

The   oh   boy   LAST   thing   she   wanted: WHEEEEEOOOOOO *oh! Another puzzle!* Her beautiful (understand, at this point) lined face may have had its days of allure but as real as it was it was still a mask, because she didn't know how to react to those puzzles in her head, so she had fixed her face to look like she knew the answers, that was important.

Hmmm hmm.

How long he had wondered, would these things last? No, *could* last, the way they were, although things seemed okay. Yet seated in a dark theater, watching a movie — an art film — a character asked a girl if she would see, and talk to him, tell him the truth, just once, one day or even one night which as the movie star hid her face in her hands and wept her confession: celery stalks at midnight.

It began as a trickle between rocks, which they followed until it widened into a creek a couple of steps across but then wider. Clear and shallow, yet widening as they walked, it became a small river into which they tossed stones, but, in their boyish competition, for the banks of the river were covered with stones and pebbles, but even with Ralph's pitching arm he couldn't throw one across. The earth rose, the air rang with the cries of natives, which surrounded them, perspiring, dank and smelling, in some sort of celebration — it was the Ganges!

Lloyd and Ralph make their way between the shouting, cheering bodies, tossing pebbles in the water, near the shore, not to hit the many people, splashing in the river . . .

Ralph looked back, behind him, over the heads of people, to where they had come from, and far away he saw a tiny raft in the middle of the water. On it a small, dark-skinned old woman sat cross-legged, and as she and her raft came closer, increasing in size, soon she was near, and getting bigger. Lloyd threw stones in the water, making an even line of splashes. Ralph had only two. How did Lloyd get so many? She was looking at Ralph, eyes direct. Angry. The sky darkened. Day became night, and her searchlight eyes fixed on him, and he was alone. She rose, stepped into and strode through the water toward him, to stand before him on the muddy river bank, far taller, glaring down: sky turned a plum color, she was ten feet tall. He raised his eyes and saw the wrinkles disappear, her muscles cable-like, rippled power: naked, firm, skin taut, taller yet, he saw up between her spread legs into her dripping, glistening red vulva, shaggy cave: muscles tense with power. Belly and full breasts seemed to boom. She radiated light, she glowed, faint blue waves surrounded her, and she despised him. Hands out, fingers curved, claw-like down, rained invectives in a guttural language upon him as he crouched, helpless, at her feet — her giant head bent, two ovals of fire and fume seethed down on him, fangs bluewhite gleaming. Ralph fell to his knees in dizziness, terror, confusion. Her animal savagery exuded organic fact: long dark hair knotted in mud and sweat, body stinking of urine, excrement. A blazing, setting sun behind her outlined her colossal bronze power, and violence. Ralph dwindled, fell on her filthy muddy feet, and toes in darkness, face buried in his hands: she kept him there, like that, her force held him there, lightning sliced white blasts lighting the scene, as thunder rocked the sky . . .

His most sustained, unrealized terror, the one that lasted the longest, was that he had, right away, seen that she was not only beautiful, but smart. And God knew that was true, and held true it seemed forever, boy it took a *lot* of living to discover how wrong he was, and stupid she had been, brains and college education just like daddy wanted, even admonishing her to get *better* grades! Ha ha ha, get it? Beautiful and smart to fall for that other fella who did little but enjoy what he wanted, and took, in a way, yes, maybe in a way like she did at home, with Ralph, who told her he loved her and she believed him, why not? He did! From the beginning in Vietnam, through the Civil Rights movement and the Nixon/Ford years, hm? Together or apart, Ralph loved her, not like that *other* guy! Unh *unh, another* guy and except for sex in secret rooms, like before, way back with that older, other guy, also married with kids, this guy stayed married, too, and would not, to her amazement, leave his wife, and children for her! Hm ha.

This in the future but there, like before in the past, she wept, and getting out of Nam the way we did, she told her ex-husband — she told Ralph about Harold, begging him to tell her, how could Harold do it? Love her and yet stay at home with his family?

"Why ask me? Why not ask your shrink?"

She lowered her eyes, and looked away, leaving it for him to interpret. Like this:

Either she didn't tell her shrink or she did and her shrink wouldn't tell her. He bet she didn't tell her.

126

Her shrink knew, Ralph realized—through his therapy—what a dummy she was, and, par for the course, wanted her to find out why. It was, in truth, not that difficult, there were *no* complications. She had put herself in the spot of being a married man's mistress, and believed his sweet-sounding lies of love, while he got some different honey than the sweets he got at home. So!

She thought she could take the cards her father dealt, go out in the world of men, and with her looks and her body play to win her game, for her! Play the game *her* way . . . so if he fucked her he would love her and thus take her away, yes!

Where she was in Ralph's heart, that dummy who, before they went to that party where his heart got broken, bought her another present—a straight up and down sizzler of a red dress to wear. And while chiding him, she loved it, laughing as she put it on or rather snaked her way into it for it fit like skin, low in front and back, spaghetti straps, and short hem above her knees, cute dimpled knees: a scarlet sheath dress, with every curve.

She tugged and turned and dipped her shoulders, look-ing long from all angles into the tall mirror, born she was, to be in that red dress, with her slender ankles, dark eyes, tawny skin, and long, curly auburn hair . . . and in the throng, beyond the crowd around the fireplace, warm hearth and laughter, out on the likewise crowded floor, to the Beatles and Stones, Ralph and his wife danced, other men turned, to look at her . . . before his eyes, emerging as from a crowd on the street, a fellow cut in with a suave smile, gave Ralph a glance with veiled eyes, and swept her across the floor, her merriment increasing, she seemed to come alive anew, in his arms, as she waved to Ralph, before disappearing among other dancers.

Where, he asked himself, later on, had they gone?

Standing, meanwhile, by the fire, listening to John Len-non's lyrics as he drank whiskey and soda, several people had gone home. Ralph gazed into the flames, feeling his face glow, and as in a montage over fire: words from a narrative in a dramatic male voice — the woman had told the police beforehand: "As we emerge from the theater, I'll be the woman in the red dress. The man at my side will be John Dillinger," feeling himself pushed, he turned, hearing a voice, it was her: they were face to face. She had never been more beautiful, or seductive, as she lied,

"I'm going for a walk with him, down to the corner . . ."
"Get some fresh air," he heard himself say.
"Yes!"

Her gaze was low, and deep, above a smile, with her dimples. Cheeks radiant. Eyes as dark as a cat's, she slipped away, her coat over her shoulders, and the red dress.

But whether what or how or even who, in the grand voyage of life what does it do, in all or in particular ways but hurt, *and so full*: rushing through him as he stood like a statue looking into the fire, deaf to the music . . . an ink drawing, a cartoon of a man at a party, standing on the hearth staring at flames with a drink in his hand, and tears in his eyes.

Ah, how else was he to be? Even after reasons named, every cause identified, for him in all being human, but to suffer . . . his full heart where she had lived was broken, and empty, all things, metabolic, violent, tragic by fire the lone man at the wheel of his ship in the bottom of his life at sea, like in Lawrence's great poem, but . . . not . . . yet: no, but oh soon enough there, in *that very beginning sense right there,* he began to change.

Later in his life he had a couple more changes, quite like this one — and just as big — they appeared identical, but the impact was not. Each awakened aspect of his previous life with, mind you, a vision of the future being enriched by the childhood of his past occurring in the middle of every day

128

by day so-called commonplace, events, it was *a lot* like going crazy. Ordinary things had terrific significance. Everything had a history. Everything mattered, *it was all important* in the lyrics, no diamonds, big cars, aw honey, they just cost money . . . little things mean a lot. Oh yes. *They* were the talismans!

For the people who don't change, and are blind to these vistas, there is no purpose in giving detail to what Ralph experienced, save that he began on the spot just after she departed, as the language of war changed from additional personnel, in re the Green Berets sent to Viet Nam, to Advisors, for the media as arm of government to position the public, set 'em up for what's to come, of course she returned, and their married life resumed its norm, at which point, or so it seemed, no one gave it much thought, although against her wishes she became an object of pleasure for her lover, she let it continue, as if Daddy didn't mind, as if Daddy said okay: L.B.J. said he'd end the war.

Ralph, not being able to say right out, for he didn't know her secret, was beginning to dream dreams in a way as if he was not just himself but somebody else, how frightening! And whether she was in his arms or someone else's, he didn't stop loving her. She knew that, understood it. So it was he thought natural for her to show up in his dreams because she lived with him within where he was, in his way unthinking going along with her until she didn't. No matter how she felt, and what she ought to do, she was who, and what she was, and she knew what she wnated, hadn't Daddy asked her, in his teasing way, with that twinkle in his eye,

"You want something, you name it. You tell me," he joked, "and I'll say okay, go get it."

Ralph made coffee for her, too, before she went to work, cleaning up afterwards. They didn't like breakfast in those days. He made her breakfast in bed on weekends, gotten used to it, although he felt certain pangs, and she had said not to spoil her — warned him, rather. *Don't* spoil me, *please,* in that tone of voice Ralph wished would stalk at midnight.

The water was warm.

She looked at him with long eyes saying no, she was going to visit her sister. She was perhaps as beautiful as ever, maybe more so . . . as a scene from a B movie to be engraved in a priceless metal, and bolted onto the front door of his memory to never forget, for Ralph told her he knew about the other guy with the wife and kids and where they lived and Ralph looked at her as she lowered her eyes, said:

"You've been busy."

"Um hm."

She stepped up into the bus, and turned back, to look at him. Sad, and guilty and a lot more but it would make no difference. Even the realization that she needed and wanted Ralph to understand didn't matter.

Floating face down he saw things—a red shovel half buried in sand, a ball with green bands. A yellow pail and small fish, slow turning seashells, shifting in currents over the white sand ocean floor. A wonderful security.

Raised his head above water to gaze at a long, wooden breakwater slanting out to sea, sunken piles and cement like the spine of a massive, primordial serpent, with a lifeguard in chair, atop a tower on the beach, seeming tiny in a colorful resort hotel world, under a vast blue sky. Ralph swam in circles, happy paddling. Raised his head, waves splashed his cheekbones, noticed a man, standing at water's edge, watching him.

The sun shifted.

Couldn't see his face.

Only part of his jaw.

Ralph swam out to sea, not going much of anywhere, little arms paddling, legs thrashing, saw a jagged shadow stretch out from the tip of the man's feet, oblique on sand. Ralph recoiled. It slid into water. He cried out. It sprang. Zigzagged: twinkled, blurred: *shot* into Ralph's soft, pink, toes.

130

By mutual agreement and of course with Ralph's help, she left him, and moved across town, into a small duplex top floor apartment in the suburbs, in fact, by luck, close to her job.

And as she took the last, little things she would need, gave Ralph a kiss at — his — front door, where he said,

"If you're in trouble and . . ." Pause. "Wait. I mean if you get, if you feel asleep, and want to wake up, think of me."

"Thank you," she murmured, wanting to go.

"Did you hear what I said?"

"*Yes!*" she lied.

Embraced him, pushed open the door and, crossing in snow to the car where her friends waited, they helped her inside, no one looking at or waving to Ralph, as he watched the car drive away.

He stepped outside, let snow fall on his upturned face. Felt good.

Every once in a while he visited her, went for walks in her neighborhood park. She couldn't believe Harold, who had said he loved her, would not leave his wife and kids. She wept a lot. Bitter tears, and he dared not talk about himself. His routine hadn't changed. His visits with her were memorable in the way he hadn't known her by his — and her — living alone, he saw how she placed belongings, like people do in first living away from home, learning where furniture, pictures, and private things belonged, hurt in that way for her, awed by her love for Harold and cut by her ignoring him. His therapist had said no sex. Ralph knew why. So in a nostalgic way, it was pleasant being with her, in the park, hurting him as never before, and only once again.

The house was white among the trees. Double glass doors slid open, between a flagstone patio and sunken living room, in which they were sitting, on a low studio couch against the wall near the fireplace. Some young, pretty suburban girls nearby on a long low upholstered sofa, drinking coffee, eating cookies, by casement windows, near the glass doors. Once in a while, in sidelong glances, looked across at Ralph, which he enjoyed. Dressed in spring colors, and cotton, as at a party, demure, he savored his thoughts.

A low wooden bannister rail divided his wife and himself from a neighboring dining area, beyond which a door opened into a hallway, with a feel of stairs, down. Heads and shoulders of people above the rail, of adults at a table, drinking mixed drinks and wine, so it was a party.

Ralph noticed a man seated near the door, who rose to his feet, and crossing towards the glass doors, turned, and looked at Ralph, who gave a start.

"What's wrong?" asked his wife.

"That man's in trouble."

Ralph stood up, crossed toward him.

Although inside, near the glass doors, in the happiness inside, and pleasant view of garden beyond the patio, the man's face loomed in close up, as his hands trembled, fingers stretched, turn pale, almost blue. The skin on his face tightened, lips and eyes elongated as if both ears were being pulled, he — was being torn in two! Ralph realized if he could peel the man's skin off, as if off an orange, the inside of the man's head would explode bones and brains and eyeballs and teeth and blood everywhere. With a groan the man dwindled, and going up steps passing the girls, Ralph confronted the man, stepping close, Ralph knelt, facing him. Their faces close, the man realized Ralph's presence, touched him. The living room filled with the man's face, lined and grim in tragedy, and fear, as balloon-sized tears slid down pale cheeks, his giant house-sized head began to nod, lips twisted into a blurred smile of sad, bitter, and unwilling farewell. Forehead tall chalk cliff.

"What is it?" Ralph asked.

The other shook his massive head, unable to speak. Ralph reached up, to touch his cheek and the man turned his face on him, its look throwing Ralph's head back for the face was petrified, and beginning to crumble, its eyes grew larger, and wider and in the far corner of each as if beginning near the ears, and coming toward the center, an inky blueblack shadow appeared, and made its first move, like a curtain, toward each iris and pupil, which trembled, and blurred as the man whimpered, fell to his knees, and reached out to Ralph, gasped,

"Help!"

"I'll go for a doctor," Ralph said, rising to his feet, and in the doorway, before rushing outside, turned.

The man had risen and stood with his feet apart, arms out, head and face straining upward. The blueblack stain in both eyes, left and right, like curtains closing across his wide, bugged, terrified eyes as each iris and pupil straining from their centers. Lips parted toward a scream.

Ralph ran down sidewalks along deserted streets passing houses, scrub fields, an occasional parked car — saw two women walking in front of two men, coming towards him, from church. The women looked at him.

"Listen," Ralph panted, "a man's dying back there! I have to find a doctor! Can you help me?"

The women looked at their husbands, and murmured *who could they call?* The husbands did not . . . *We're very sorry* . . .

Ralph ran on, encountering other married couples or sweethearts who were sorry, *they didn't know,* and on he ran, until at last a young woman, alone, who looked intelligent, with questions in her eyes, asked him what was wrong?

With force he repeated the message, and she understood it, she, seeming to be a knowing person, he thought, he thought he saw a look in her eyes — she might be able —

"We have to work *fast!*" he snarled: "this man *has been poisoned!*"

Her intelligent eyes turned inward, and Ralph watched her search . . . but she found no answers it was all streets and fields he had run beyond the point of no return. They didn't know. Nobody knew, and the young woman's eyes returned to his, in sadness, and in regret and puzzled in his memory, he ran on.

And began to live by himself—alone—in earnest, without her, and not knowing how, he began all over. Body as if asleep, was impotent for many weeks, and waking one morning amid rumpled sheets, felt infantile, pulled and tugged a soft blanket, hugged it close, in a crib, feeling himself in his crib, closed his eyes, and slept, waking aware of air on his cheek . . . phoned his therapist who said keep a diary, he did. Beside his bed, notated, *"Being reborn."*

Very very few understood, the long, isolate voyage, never knowing it would happen again during Watergate, and again during the last term of the Puppet President Movie Star, deepest shock and hurt he returned to the first point, the original location of peace, discovery, wonder, comfort and safety, to begin anew. To grow and learn many things, one of which would be that none but true lovers and dreamers who had suffered loss would change, few others would dare. Say *none*. Not the big, straight up and down pure change, affecting everything, to love others as never before, to enjoy yourself to like what you were, eager to become what you would, alone until by chance someone appeared—poet, lover, dreamer . . . sky blue, warm, breezy day. She, there. Again.

They walked into the water, and began to swim toward what appeared the other side, a grassy rise against the sky. And on reaching it, walked up on the shore, through tall reeds and grass onto familiar footpaths.

Leading to other waterways and inlets, across which they swam, a few lagoons, until they came to a larger place, where they walked between trees which got thicker, and were in periods in darkness, where they moved with care, through ferns and bushes. So it was dark as they stepped into water again, and swimming was strange and spooky, and more

134

difficult, for it thickened, began to cling like mud. With bits of wood, and paper—debris, in it. There seemed no end to swimming. He tired.

"How are you doing?" he asked her.

"Okay," she said. Better swimmer.

"I hope I can make it."

"It can't be much further."

"Hope so."

He knew—both knew, there was no turning back, but as his arms and legs began to stiffen, he was afraid, and began a heavy sort of dog paddle. A voice called out, was it just ahead? Soon Ralph's feet touched bottom, and he and his wife clambered up a muddy slope to a flat, grassy area and rested.

They got to their feet, though, and entered a jungle much more dense than before, and slow going. Ralph stayed close by her, with the blonde artist and his wife close behind, and the others following them. In the afternoon they arrived at the top of a cliff. Ralph stood, gazing over, perceiving a girl in wet rags, climbing up.

"Let's go down!" he cried, and led the way, passing the girl—

"What's it like?" Ralph asked her.

She tilted her head, he followed the direction to a group of people swimming in a very muddy lake at the foot of stick houses with thatch roofs on platforms, standing near the shore. The people seemed to be enjoying themselves.

"It's fun!"

Ralph and his wife, and the blonde artist and his wife who had appeared joined the people swimming, but the people were too rough, noisy, coarse, animal-like, splashing and ducking, but no sooner than they were away from them they were swimming across endless arrangements of waterways, lagoons, inlets between narrow fingers of land covered by tall, dense reed forests, like sugarcane. But the water was clear, and the sky as blue as the high sunny days of before, and they swam out into a clearwater lake where they in part floated for it was so clear and shallow, until they came onto land, and so it went, crossing one narrow waterway after another until they came to a large island.

The ground was hard, and gray, packed as if pounded, and dusty, palm trees beaten husks and the grass, too, and bushes: dry, split, frayed beside beaten, dusty gray dirt paths.

The whole island seemed that way, mean, stripped, and barren. Trees carved with graffiti and sadistic slashes, as they continued walking, and arriving at some deserted grass huts, the sky was white. Ralph and his wife were alone.

He was depressed, and frightened.

Heard the sound of angry laughing men, as they came to a clearing, saw unshaven, dirty white men in undershirts and torn khakis, milling around, drinking from cans of beer.

They passed them unnoticed, and descended a steep, very dusty, thus hard and slippery cliff, into a dry, ripped bamboo, torn grass village of straw shacks. Gray dirt between as hard as concrete.

And that was the place where they were, on the edge, just outside it, as the days and nights went by, and late one afternoon, as they stood outside by the corner of their shack, Ralph and his wife close together, his arm over her shoulder, hers around his waist as she thought her thoughts and rather gazing at the village, dry husks of palm trees, tall dry weeds and matted grass, Ralph too in reverie, gazing out beyond the village—cried,

"Look!"

"What is it?" she asked, in truth distracted.

Through the dry, shattered jungle Ralph saw the twinkle of a clearwater inlet. Light came into his eyes, his lips parted. He reached for her, but she told him to wait.

So Ralph fell still, and looking again at the twinkling water, through the dust in jungle grayness, saw a ray of sunlight reveal the vista of a lush, emerald green valley and a dark green frog!

136

"I'm going swimming," she said, stepping away.

"Stay!" Ralph cried. "See the frog in the emerald valley?"

"I'll be back," she murmured, with a smile, and walked into the jungle.

Ralph, missing her, yet stunned, remained staring into the full green lilypads and budding flowers, leaves, and the still, dark green frog, in the ray of sunlight in the heart of the emerald valley. Ralph took a step or two toward it, as among the constant traffic of passing half-naked, unshaven men in their faded fatigues — these veterans, among them appeared a young man, with sympathetic eyes, who gazed at Ralph.

She returned, limping, being helped by one of the men, with the snout of a pig. Fell into Ralph's arms, had broken her foot. Her upturned face damp, and pale, grim with pain. Beyond them Ralph noticed the young man with understanding eyes — he could trust him. She said,

"I have to go back."

"Go back?" Ralph exclaimed. "Go *BACK*?" Overwhelmed, held her in his arms. "Can't you see how far we've come? How *far* it's been? And LOOK, *THERE!*" Pointing to the clear, fresh water, the deep, deep green valley and the frog. "Can't you see?"

"You go," she said, as if resolute. "I know you want to . . . you must . . ."

Her foot and ankle dark blue, swollen. Ralph furious, heartbroken. "Go BACK! You can't swim with that!"

"I'll make it," she said, expression grave, as men with those snouts began to weave a thatch litter, to carry her. So. She was going away. Ralph felt himself slant out in separation, alone, and in hurt and anger,

"Your foot, your Goddamned FOOT! Why in all we've gone through, after ALL THIS DISTANCE, YOU DID THIS! *WHY? WHY?*"

Raised both his fists, and cursed.

"I'll meet you," she said, from afar. He threw out his arms—

"WHERE? *How will you know?*"

"I don't know," her voice diminishing, he last saw her face, so vivid in his life begin to fade, as he heard her voice, so soft—afar—"Goodbye. I'll be there."

Statue Ralph, frozen, hands out.

Would chase her wherever she went, had gone at her side with her in his heart, her voice came from a hollowness—

"You go . . . go."

He turned, and looked at the frog in the emerald valley. *Go alone to Paradise?*

Buried his face in his hands, and wept.

As the sympathetic man spoke with his eyes of understanding, and Ralph's wife was helped onto the litter by the pig men, who raised and carried her into the jungle.

Waking early on some mornings, his pillow damp from tears, his loneliness had such force it terrified him, and in bed, sniffled, wiped his eyes, in predawn darkness, curled up under the covers, his face in his hands, not knowing what to do, he wept, and dozed, slept deep. Woke. Got up. Began the day.

As he shaved he saw in the mirror that his face was different: certain lines that had been on his forehead were gone. Eyes so clear, like glass. Gaze open, direct. Yet searching. Why? Trying to see.

Made it to work. Punched in. Traffic dispatcher for a shipping firm, checked arrivals and departures. Guys on the job knew she'd left him. They thought Ralph was doing pretty good. Was seeing a shrink, well, that's what he would do. Me, no. But Ralph, yeah. That kind of guy.

His strength was within his vulnerability, with the sharp sparkle-glow of creative, inquisitive children in his eyes. His personality was patient, reflective yet open and forward moving. Without knowing it people saw themselves in him because

138

he knew what and where he was, he was vivid, real, dreamlike. Life was new, frightening, irresistible—magnetic, with astonishing surprises—it became clear right away—that were part of the process: even its reward. Taste, touch, smell, sound and vision reawakened childish responses, to as if ease his fading, former identity—as he died on the way into the sunlight, renewing.

On the corner of his windowsill, where his cat Dizzy played with the curtain, in that spot of sunlight as Ralph sat up in bed, in the morning, and feeling new, and free, gazed, fascinated, at the slow, slow changing patch of sun. He was happy, because it was living there before his eyes, and it was changing, causing him to smile, as happy as a trusting boy.

This consistent no-clock/calendar experience of his senses and spirit, with therapy gave him added dimension which no one could understand, and only he, approaching early middle age, in his mythic Pilgrim-self, seeing the world as never before, heard, listened for example, to Mozart with a spectacular sensitivity. At a concert, having heard a violin concerto, went at intermission to thank the performer, and whilst she signed his program—in that tiny room, jammed with other fans—he asked her if she had in the beginning of the second movement, heard and elaborated on Mozart's *Requiem*, for it sounded spontaneous, or was it written that way?

"It was written that way," she responded, with that refreshing candor performing artists so enjoy *after* performance. Yet she perceived that she was being heard in a complete sense, not just in passing, so her voice was a shade different, saying, "The *Requiem* runs through a lot of his works."

"That's true," Ralph agreed. "From his First Symphony, where it began."

"Are you a musician?"

"No," in deference.

And departing from the room, glanced back, to see her in conversation with an admiring fellow in a dark blue suit, white silk scarf. Ralph walked down stairs, back to his seat for the second half of the concert, happy at being alone. But sad. Sad.

So open to continuing change, to so many aspects of life, who could know? Meaning where was she who did, but no. Who had wanted to, and discovered how — but no. Each would in their way, not his, beginning to get accustomed to himself, he'd never know another woman in that expectant way, but only in a way of gambit, for every variety of change changed every variety of human being in the many ways people will, and will not, change. So with that intuitive lead he visited a friend's son in prison, by way of obligation but in part not for he liked the young man, and was sad that fate and the law had combined for such luck.

In conversation which did not come as easy as Ralph had expected, the warm, easygoing fellow had become distrustful, and depressed, appeared hostile with Ralph who asked him if he kept a diary?

"No. You want me to write poetry?" Sardonic amusement. "I know a guy here who writes poetry, and he's *good.* You should meet him. I mean it."

Okay, Ralph thought, and to be amiable, by way of sustaining friendship, told him to tell the other inmate to send him some poetry . . . well, the fellow did.

Two long poems on blue lined paper, in the same harmonies and rhythms as Poe, you could even say the guy imitated Poe, and you'd be right *but!* So what? It had come from Poe but was *not* Poe, it was *the poet* writing two long poems of love, for and toward a mysterious young lady during all these inside years, from her teens! In his suffering, and loneliness, a poet, a dreamer he knew what unhappiness was, and because he didn't know much about happiness save in gratification and mother-warmth, he presented a personality of weary, edgy patience, and a hostile, even antagonistic, superior, quiet attitude. He could read and write and speak his mind, and as he had learned long ago, would not be drawn

140

into the drowning whirl of the loathsome hatred that ignorant people have for each other: unreported cause for many a murder or stabbing, not to mention the violent madness of locked up bodies.

Teachers spoke of him in low tones, Ralph heard, long after. They said he copied Edgar Allan Poe, which gave Ralph a laugh. Who hasn't? Part of growing up is copying Poe: to enter life's mystery, boys and girls all over the world copied Poe.

And William Blake.

One day Ralph visited his friend's son and the poet together, for a study not only in character difference, but for a hint of the range of different personalities behind the walls of U.S. prisons which, Ralph gathered in the many varied days and nights ahead, went unreported in *total* silence, because world news was involved in *event,* not in the variety and quality of human character.

His poems based on Poe were the complete testament of his love for the girl, and too, his understanding of her, for she was by no means simple, or superficial . . . in his use of Poe he used Poe's feel for darkness, danger, inevitable doom, and adventure and that ever beautiful, eternal, sublime awareness, of romantic loss of the beloved.

Ralph visited again.

They sat in the Visiting Room, facing each other across a small table, one of several such tables in a row, where other couples likewise sat, with a guard at either end.

Ralph complimented him on the poems, and they talked a little about Poe, and early influences. Ralph mentioning, for example, Kipling.

"The racist."

"Yes," Ralph said. "But the rhythms, Kipling's rhyme structure influenced at least three generations of creative people in the west — and east. Kipling was the inspiration for England in both wars."

"You like Kipling," the poet smiled.

"I did more than do. My mother and father read Kipling out loud to us." Ralph checked himself, for he was there, on the sofa with his sister, cookies and milk, while his father read *Kim*, the greatest novel of espionage ever written, a denied masterpiece that had influence on world history: Philby's father, a T. E. Lawrence-styled romantic adventurer, named his son Kim, after that book.

"Well," the poet said, seeing Ralph in reverie, "you'd better go. I don't want to keep you."

"You're not keeping me," Ralph smiled. "These things mean a lot to me. I can't help reflect on them . . . shall I tell you how my mother loved Poe, walked round our house quoting *Annabel Lee?*"

" ' 'Twas many and many a year ago,' " the poet began, his eyes on his visitor—

" 'In a kingdom by the sea.' " Ralph said, his eyes likewise.

And together—

> "There lived a maiden whom you may know
> By the name of Annabel Lee."

The way the walls of the room tapered to institutional infinity, in a smell of something like cotton, baking bread and what, *Vicks?* made Ralph a little giddy, in the sudden, captivating return to childhood—denim, the laundry! On the line, drying! In the back yard near the garage, by the lilies—the little bench from grandfather's porch, on nice days, yes! If he was sick, she bundled him up and let him sit on the bench in the sun, with a warning finger: as the sun's shadow touched the violets by the corner of the house, in he comes! *Yes!* She liked to bake bread in the afternoon . . .

The young man facing Ralph watched him with sharp, intense eyes, for he was learning something about somebody else and he knew, as people do, that it was that that was going on. The beginning of a smile rippled into curiosity for an expression of interest: as Ralph asked,

"May I bring you anything?"

"No thank you," the other answered. "I have all I need." Pause. "Tell me about yourself. You mentioned, in your last letter, that you had written something, about artistic criticism? for a magazine or newspaper?"

"Ah yes, I forgot. Here." Passing it over. "Let me know what you think. I mean, write me."

"What do you do?"

"I'm a dispatcher for World Over van lines, a moving company. We did a job for a museum and I wrote something about it — for the company's newsletter."

"About the moving job?"

"No, about the paintings we moved."

"Oh! And what were they?"

"Couple of Rembrandts, Matisses, early Impressionists, and work unseen in the west, from museums in Russia."

"Because of Gorbachev, do you think?"

"Yes."

"Where was it sent?"

"To Los Angeles."

"I see."

Glancing at it. Ralph —

"I brought it to let you know, that I like your work not just as, " he paused. "As someone," he gestured, "who is just a person, and — " realized he had done something well-meaning but stupid, " — that I know what good work is, not just to pat you on the shoulder, and say, 'Well done.' " Pause. "I didn't mean it to be highbrow," angry at himself. "Besides, the editor made some changes."

"Where did he make those changes?" the poet asked, eyes wide, hard. "Tell me. Let me read it, and you tell me. I want to be a writer! I must know these things! Will you help me?"

"Sure! Read it, and let me know what you think, first."

"I see," the poet — amused — smiled. "You want me to do *my* homework." Pause. "May I ask you something?"

"Sure."

"If anything happens to me, you can contact my brother. Here is his address."

From a small notebook handed Ralph a page, which Ralph read and slipped into shirt pocket.

"What could happen to you?"

"I don't know, but it might," with an odd, ambiguous expression, the future always uncertain behind bars. "In here, anything may happen."

Ralph took from his wallet a business card, handing it over. Watching the other read it, and say

"Thank you."

"You're welcome," Ralph replied, and rose to his feet as did the other man, where they shook hands. In his secret way Ralph was sad.

"You don't need to feel sad," smiled the prisoner. "I see in your expression that you do, but you don't need to. I have been in Keeplock for a few weeks, but I am out, and back in population. I will survive and in my way, perhaps I will even be happy."

"I hope so."

"Thank you again for everything."

"My pleasure."

"Will you come again?"

"Of course."

"*Good!*"

"Take care!"

"You have a *safe* trip home!"

In the taxi going home — deeper into the filth of the decaying city, accumulating as they got closer and closer —

144

Ralph let himself open up and welcome the imprisoned poet into his life.

On arriving home, he re-read the long love poems, and having just been in his company, realized again how good they were, and some slight changes that should be made, wondering once again where he could get them published or, maybe get it printed on his own, and—well, in any event, write a brief introduction.

He had a dream that night which he understood was lost in waking up to a ringing telephone, and answering and talking with a new friend about seeing a movie, yes yes, noting the new information on a pad on his nightstand, said,

"I just had a dream, but can't remember it!"

"Because I phoned you!" cried the woman.

He laughed.

"Does it matter?" she asked. "I'll bet it does."

"It might," he said. "Bye."

"Bye . . ."

In bed, alone, he stared long into darkness.

Next day at work, the morning paper belonging to one of the guys, opened to the entertainment section and had, in the HBO listing, something that caught his eye, so he paused to read, glancing down at Warren Oates in *Dillinger.*

Ralph stood there, in the job office, surrounded by the dispatcher's world of interstate and overseas trucking, with no expression on his face, letting the memory filter down into its place where it would be met by its duplicate on an upward rise, from where it had been from the outset, and in the soft explosion of their union, its new life would find new connections belonging to only it, and settle in where it belonged, and in that way of kinship Ralph became aware that in a shape he had yet to discover, he was being passed a piece of information, and like a pebble against a glass window, he remembered his dream: a poem, which on crossing the office, sitting at his desk and with paper and pencil, he felt he was in high school, as he wrote:

In the field of Love I found
A circle lying on the ground.
A circle! Round, complete
Lying perfect at my feet.

At that same desk a week or so later, while Ralph looked up the telephone number of a midwestern freight transfer company, Alice returned from lunch, punched in and, sitting at her desk, glanced at him, peering at yellow pages.

"Want some help?"

"No, thanks."

The phone rang.

"I've got it," he said, and in a slight start the phone operator said he had a collect call from an inmate at a correction facility. Would he accept?

"Yes."

The voice which from the other end followed was unclear, and in a suspense, Ralph bewildered until he recognized it, and the prisoner was saying—

"She left me. She's gone."

"How do you know? Did she write, or—"

"No. I phoned her. She told me."

"I'm sorry."

"What will I do?"

"You must help, and take care of yourself. Let her go."

"How do I do that? I love her!"

"But she does not love you. She's gone. It's you you must turn to."

"She used me!"

146

"Why? How?"

"I don't know!" Pause. "She said she loved me, and it felt like she used me, she is using me!"

"Do you want to tell me? Did she say things about you?"

"Yes!"

Ralph leaned forward, tense.

"Do you think she loved the illusion of you, safe from a distance, but up close, the real you, no?"

Breath caught. "Maybe!"

"She made you into something you're not?"

"Yes. I think she did that."

"Because you were getting too close?"

"Maybe."

Silence for reactions.

Confined to his cell in Keeplock, 23 hours a day, allowed to make one call a week, which was to her, after a few weeks she couldn't take that intensity.

"All right, let her go. In the end she wants to be away from you, not close, no matter what she says. Let her go."

". . . How do I?"

"In yourself, open up and tell her, inside yourself: say, Go from me! *Go!*"

"Yes. Maybe."

"Let her go. You're the one. Let the feelings you had for her dissolve in the emptiness she leaves in you, and pay no attention. It won't be easy. You gave her your imagination in your poetry, in your thoughts and dreams, along with your love. But save all that for yourself. You will need it. Want it."

"I'm not sure I understand, but maybe I do. It sounds good."

"Let's give you some love. You are the poet, the dreamer, the one who cares. You in truth are the strong one, and must take care of yourself, without any illusions, to be alone, in your change."

"But it will be difficult, won't it?"

"The most difficult of all things, but the pain won't last forever, and you'll know right away. Focus on what *you* want, and need. Be aware of *your*self. You. If you need me, call me at home. I'm more free there, and I pay my own phone bill."

Amusement. "I see. Yes, your boss will pay this. I'm sorry, but thank you. I appreciate this. Your words are good. I must go."

"Keep in touch."

"I will."

Ralph set the receiver down, slow, with care, and feeling pale, looked across the room.

"How did I do?" he asked.

"You were *great!*" Alice said, wide-eyed. "Was this the fella you mentioned?"

"Yes."

She rose, and crossed the room to stand, and look down at him. Put her hand on his shoulder, and by her standing at his side, being so close, her touch caused Ralph to lower his head in reflection yet to raise it, and gaze up at her, saying,

"His girlfriend left him."

On returning home that evening, found a note from the prisoner saying he had enjoyed the article in the newsletter. With thanks, and in Arabic, his name, and a few words Ralph didn't understand, above the word, in English, beneath his name — *Peace.*

Several days later Ralph received a note from the same gentleman, written in blue ball-point pen, on blue lined paper, which read:

My Friend Ralph,

Your words were appreciated. They were good.
Thank very much. In Peace.

(signature)

And about a week later, in the mail, on a square, blue lined page from a pad, were three short poems that told the story, all the story, and even gave the location, and indeed the prayer. Typed, each with a title, and in the right margin, how he wanted them to be regarded.

COME BACK PURPLE LETTER

personal

She sits there avidly in that old
worn out desk   in the middle drawer
isolate and empty   while I merely think of
her all night long wondering if she
knows   but I know she does not   yet I
wonder if she realizes the darkness and
the black arms of another cold and endless
night   I can't help but wonder . . .
as I drift off to sleep.

PERVERTED

poem

Ugly emetic dangerous is
The act of forbidden
Thoughts in the land of
Forbidden justice among
The people of forbidden
perverts.

A PRAYER OF HOPE

By the Dawn and the birds that fly
By the stars as they cover the sky
By the veil and the Thirty Days
By the thought and the one who says
By all these things I sit to cry
Allah my Lord don't pass me by.

The Rose

The Red Rose is a symbol of love. The White Rose is a symbol of a kiss. In this world there are many white roses, but yet not enough red roses. I can give you my white rose, but you can walk away without it. But in my heart you will always carry my red rose.

James Welsher
Wyoming Correctional Facility
88CO514
P.O. Box 501
Attica NY 14011-050X

for Debora

IN CLASS, standing before the men, with the blackboard behind him, a desk and chair to one side, he gazed at the opposite wall which, depending on which prison he was in, had colorful posters, bulletin boards or windows through which he saw, beyond tall barbed-wire topped chainlink fences, rolling hills of neighboring farms: a view from the medium security joints, where the guards were bored, hostile, and picky on details as he cleared security before being escorted to classrooms.

Or the big, ugly Maximum Security prisons, with their vast, high walls, gun towers, long corridors (that defined

151

tunnel vision), and always the dim, grim, gray, drawn faces
and expressions male and female guards on guard, keepers
of the kept, wherever he went and he went wherever he could,
like Johnny Appleseed, looking for talent, scattering seeds
to grow trees inside heads so after he'd gone, in the wilderness
of the future, somewhere, some way, pen or pencil might con-
nect with paper, in a poem.

Prison poetry often appeared in spontaneous first draft
where from common inspiration it remained as an expression of its author, for its destiny or, once in a while, to show
up in writing or poetry workshops, inside the prison, and
stayed, ready for reading aloud, until a couple of guys over
by the window, hot in conversation about cars, one of them,
announcing, as his buddies gave him soft punches saying *go
ahead,* with sad eyes and a tense expression, manslaughter,
while another fellow — like the rest — waited, as teacher caught
the eye of a quiet young man seated near the corner, who
raised his hand.

"Yes?" Teacher.

"I have a poem."

"Do you want to read it?"

"Well, yeah. Unh huh."

"Great!"

Young, pale, shy. Average build, an American kid, the
back of his neck seeming extra vulnerable, routine with inmates. Teacher smart enough not to observe too close the
young man's body, in that evil world of locked-up flesh. He
would save his watching people pleasure for the street.

So, winding up the discussion on a short story, teacher
and the guys turned to the quiet inmate, yet teacher still involved in the story: the author (inmate) had gotten drunk at
a party, and on the way home began to drive fast, having
a souped-up vintage model such-and-such car from year so-
and-so going top speed over a hundred fell asleep, woke to
avoid a tree, and back on the highway again fell asleep to
wake and just miss a shoulder guard rail, regained the road

to fall asleep to wake in collision with a car in front with people inside: the injuries had been severe. Teacher thinking about falling asleep and waking up to fall asleep to wake up in the Smirnoff hit, while the other read his poem, *The Rose,* self-conscious, and as is the case in prison classrooms, while work is read, all are quiet.

"The Red Rose is a symbol of love. The White Rose is a symbol of a kiss. In this world there are many white roses, but yet not enough red roses. I can give you my white rose, but you can walk away without it. But in my heart you will always carry my red rose."

Following auto collision, near death and driver guilt (which in prison's turmoil the driver could just comprehend) teacher almost missed *The Rose,* but heard enough, *was* mystified, and crossing the room toward the poet, faced him, placing the driver in memory: looked into the face of the poet, seated in that student's desk chair, looking back at him, in apprehension, as teacher said,

"That was beautiful," in he thought a little too much of a matter of fact tone of voice, so turned, looked at the other guys, seated in their chairs, and, the way teachers say everywhere said: "but before we discuss it, would you like to hear it again?" Thinking,

I would.

Yeah, sure! Unh huh! Okay! Yeah!

The inmate poet a little embarrassed, surprised, not used to this, shifted in his chair, gripped the page of blue-lined paper with both hands, peered in, and began to read—

"Louder, please."

Raised his voice.

"The Red Rose is a symbol of love. The White Rose is a symbol of a kiss. In this world there are many white roses, but yet not enough red roses. I can give you my white rose, but you can walk away without it. But in my heart you will always carry my red rose."

Guys saw their teacher smiling. Looking at him in their

153

open way, for masks are lowered a little, in prison writing workshops, creative inmates wonder what teacher (who in this instance was a writer), what would he do, or say, next?

Teacher knew that, too, and gave everyone a chance to speak, urged 'em to respond to work . . .

Unlike the response to the driver's story, where there was animated discussion, on *The Rose* all agreed it was good, it was warm, loving, kind, sad, and, he made clear, like the *real* mysteries in life and love, *not* so easy to understand.

Oh yes, their expressions said, as they sat, silent, impressed by him as he looked at them, one by one, until he reached the poet, to whom he said,

"Good. That's *good!*"

In the motel that evening, in conversation with his girlfriend, wished he had a copy of *The Rose* to read to her, amazed that he couldn't remember it, save its red rose/white rose interplay, being different from other poems although of course the same, yet not, for it seemed apart, distinct.

They had come up from the city to visit her brother, and to help cover expenses he did a couple of workshops in the local medium security prison. A small college nearby had a program, where a few other teachers worked inside, too. Her brother knew the education supervisor . . .

So teacher made some phone calls, and at length spoke to a woman who taught composition to that same group he had been with, and recognized his description of that young inmate. Teacher, at this point had done a lot of talking, and realized he had to have that poem, and to his astonishment heared himself beg her to have the guy make a copy and bring it into class on Friday.

"Oh yes, I'd be delighted to," she said, to his embarrassment. "I'll talk to him tomorrow. What is —"

"I've got to have it."

" — the title?"

"*The Rose.*"

154

"Aw that's nice. He'll be pleased you're interested."

So on Friday the young inmate handed teacher a copy of *The Rose,* handwritten, ball point pen, on blue lined paper.

Teacher happy. "Thank you!" Pause. "Put your name and address on it." Smiled.

The young poet did.

As teacher had stood in front of him, and said, "Good. That's *good!*" the inmate's eyes had brightened, in a way that caused his features to soften, his lips to part, as his gaze lifted to meet the eyes of the teacher, and saw what he wanted to see: a man who saw that the two roses were his gift to the girl he loved: one she could walk away from, but in *his* heart she would always carry *the red rose of his heart,* in *HER* heart! *It was the absolute implication!* And just as the teacher had emphasized *"Good!"* after saying "Good," on approval of the poem, the expression on the young man's face warmed, for at last someone knew what love was, and might see his heart in her heart, in his, thus he lowered his eyes, yet raised them again, to meet the teacher's.

"Thank you."

Not used to this, no, not at all. Stared at the floor, as the teacher folded the poem, inserted it into a folder in his valise. The young man placed his hands in his lap, color rising in his cheeks . . .

Printed January 1991 in Santa Barbara & Ann Arbor
for the Black Sparrow Press by Graham Mackintosh
& Edwards Brothers Inc. Text set in Baskerville by
Words Worth. Design by Barbara Martin. This edition
is published in paper wrappers; there are 200 hardcover
trade copies; 125 hardcover copies have been numbered
& signed by the author; & 26 lettered copies are
handbound in boards by Earle Gray each signed & with
an original drawing by Fielding Dawson.

Photo: Mimi Fronczak

FIELDING DAWSON was born in New York in 1930. Grew up in the midwest, went to Black Mountain College from 1949 until 1953 when he was drafted. After serving in the Army he settled in New York, where except for travelling he still lives. The author of 19 published books, a member of P.E.N. and Chairman of the P.E.N. Prison Writing Committee, he is an exhibiting artist, a Pantheon author, and belongs to the Democratic Socialists of America.